The Dying God & Other Stories

S.M. Carrière

First published 2010 by S.M. Carrière.

Paperback Edition published 2011 by S.M. Carrière.

Interior design by Éric Desmarais.

ISBN: 978-0-9938509-9-8

http://www.smcarriere.com

Acknowledgments

Once upon a time, there was a little girl who would sit alone in the shade and scribble silly little snippets of stories. Never once did she dream that it could ever turn into anything real, let alone something others might enjoy. But she would read these bits and pieces to her mother and grandmother, who never once laughed at them (even though they were laughably terrible). And so that little girl kept writing. Then, on a whim, that girl decided to create a small collection of some of her silly little stories and offer them to the world. To her surprise, the world also did not laugh.

And this little anthology would not have existed without the support of everyone who, along the way, did not laugh, but instead offered words of encouragement, help and suggestions for improvement. For my mother and grandmother, who bore my early readings with the patience of the most saintly amongst us, to my friends who never once roll their eyes at me, to the greater writing community in Ottawa, where I made my debut as an author, all of whom offered nothing but openness and gentle encouragement. As someone who was so used to being run down for her weird mind, this acceptance and encouragement still, to this day, blows me away.

I want to acknowledge everyone I've met along the way whose kindness, encouragement and joy gave that terrified, lonely little girl the courage to share her stories. Though there are too many of you to name, I know that you know who you are. Thank you for being wonderful. I hope you like this small collection of art, poems and stories I wrote for you.

For Grandma

Table of Contents

Do You Believe?

I was sitting in the sun,
Enjoying its bright warmth,
When a shadow swept overhead,
And I opened up my eyes to spy
A Roc, red of wing and gold of eye.

'Climb on, my friend,' said he,
'There are forgotten things,
That you must needs to see.'
Enchanted, I climbed aboard,
And with a leap and rustling wing, went skyward.

'Look down,' he said.
'Tell me all that you can see.'
'Why, my house,' cried I.
'My garden, my chair, the brook behind the lee,
And, of course, my most favourite tree.'

No sooner had I spoke,
Than that very tree turned its trunk
And waved up at me,
With great sweeping arms, shaped like greaves,
Made of living wood, and fingers of leaves.

'Oh my,' gasped I,
And we climbed higher, up into the sky.
The ground below turned
A patchwork of green and grey,
As the sky faded to the ending colours of the day.

Into the clouds we rose,
Whereupon a Sylph offered her hand.
A giggle, and she was gone,
Riding the winds without a care,
While her sisters played havoc with my hair.

A dip of steady wing,
And we were gliding down again,
O'er plains of tall grasses
That rippled like waves as faeries fluttered by.
A herd then caught my eye. 'Unicorns!' cried I.

Overland we glided still,
Until we came across a marsh,
Whereupon the Roc began to climb.
I asked, 'Why?' He cocked his head and said, 'Beware,'
'Jenny Greenteeth lives there.'

Higher still across the hills
And up a mountainside,
Until we came to the ice and snow;
Yeti's home, his shaggy fur a perfect fit,
And hard to find, for it is more afraid of you than you are of it!

Higher still, until faced with sheer cliff,
Whereupon the Roc wheeled away,
Here even majestic Rocs fear to fly,
Refusing to climb the rocky steep.
Here, I was told, was the mighty dragon's keep.

Down we went again,
O'er hill and valley and glen,
Until we reached the shore,
Where Selkies bathed in the warmth of the sun,
And mermaids waved, one by one.

We skimmed the waves awhile,
Enjoying the scent and spray,
And guided by little men who rode fish that flew,
When the Roc titled suddenly to the side,
To avoid a sea-serpent's jaws, spread wide.

With a screech and desperate flapping
We were up again and away.
Higher and higher we climbed once more,
Back to Sylph and cloud,
When suddenly the Roc's wings were bowed.

Down we plunged, down and down.
I felt certain we were to crash,
When my host spread his wings once more,
And circled lazily, as if it didn't happen,
And then I saw my house again.

I awoke with a start, sitting in my chair,
With naught to show but a frightful tangle of hair.
A glimmer and a tinkle turned my head,
But I spied nothing more than a toadstool.
Then remembered, Faeries sit there in the evening cool.

I frowned. Could it all have been a dream?
That I had seen what I had seen,
I spied a Unicorn herd, and Sylphs, Mermaids, the monster?
I saw an eagle, and then did I perceive
A familiar voice that said: 'So, my friend, now do you believe?'

Diary of a Veteran

I know you will never believe this. Not in a million years will you believe what I have seen and am now relaying to you. I'm telling you all the same.

It will probably be many years after my death that you are reading this. I am an old man now, and no one cares about the memories of old men in this day and age. It's all about instant messaging and the latest gadget now. No one cares about the past anymore.

This is something everyone should know. It's something that we all knew as children, I think, but have since forgotten and dismissed, as if we somehow outgrew the truth. But this truth, the truth that all children know, we must once again learn to accept. That truth is simple, and it is this:

Magic exists.

There now, I've said it. Go on, laugh. I know you want to. Laugh at this foolish, doddering old man who has lost his mind. Let me tell you, my mind is as sharp as it ever was, even if my hands shake and I can only shuffle around with the aid of a walker. I'll tell you this too: the last laugh will be on me.

I used to be like you once. I only believed in what I could see and hear, taste and touch. I would scoff at people who told me all the stories about faeries and other things that sounded silly. 'Show me the proof,' I would say. 'Show me this winged creature you have on your shoulder. Then I'll believe you.'

I was a fool. And so are you.

The truth is, we all get blind as we get older. We forget all the things that do not make sense; but children just intuitively know. We dismiss everything as false; guilty until proven innocent. I had my eyes opened, oh so long ago. I'm telling you about it so that you, too, can finally see again.

There is nothing left now, but for to begin. So, here I go. Try to keep an open mind. I know it's difficult for your sort. Kids these days.

I was sixteen when I signed up to fight. I was nothing more than a Yankee boy with grand ideas of adventure and heroism. Let me tell you, there is nothing heroic about war. It's loud and bloody and hard. You kill people in war, people with families and futures who, just like you, are fighting for what they believe in.

You watch your friends die around you, sometimes on you as little bits of meaty pulp. You eat the brains of the guy in front of you in war, when his head is blown wide open by a bullet or three. Stupid Tommy. I told him to wear his helmet. He never listened. Limeys, they're all the same.

I was fighting in Holland when I was hit by a shell. Well, sort of. Enough that it sent me flying, in any case. Little Bobbit caught the worst of it. I can't remember his real name anymore. We just called him Bobbit. He was blown into tiny little pieces. My last recollection of that fight was a big bright light, a loud sound, and then silence. I saw the silhouette of Bobbit fly apart before I hit the ground and blacked out.

I couldn't tell you how long I was out for. Could've been days. Could've been months, but I wasn't in no military hospital when I woke up. Wasn't still on the field either. I was on a bed. Well, a thin mattress on a low bench. It was dark when I woke up, and the air was thick and smoky, but cool.

I could hear people talking. There was laughter somewhere outside. I frowned and tried to move, only to find that I had been bandaged up tight, like a bloody mummy in a museum. The only thing I could move was my head, so I did just that, trying to figure out where the hell I was.

I couldn't see squat, except one window that opened out into a night sky. It was filled with constellations I've never seen before. The window itself was open to the elements, and the windowsill was nothing more than daubed mud that was designed to smooth out the edges of the wattle that made up the walls. Never seen nothing like it before, but I was too tired and out of it to do much wondering.

The smoke, I remember, was coming from a bowl near the foot of my bed. It was sweet smelling and I'm sure it was that smoke that was making me as drowsy as I was. In any case, I didn't have the strength to fight it, so I just let myself fall back to sleep.

I only have patchy memories of the first part of my recovery; hazy, vague things that tell me almost nothing about that time, so I'll spare you those particular recollections. When I finally woke up with a clear head, it was midmorning. There were birds singing somewhere. It wasn't any birdsong I'd ever heard before.

I looked down. I was covered in woollen blankets, and the bowl at the end of my bed was no longer smoking. The air inside was clear and cool and smelled incredible – like grass and rich, moist earth, and flowers. After the smell of gas and oil and metal and unwashed bodies of the trenches, this was heaven.

In fact, I thought I was in heaven, that I had died and some poor angel had stitched my soul back together. Ain't no-one's soul without holes in it when you've fought a war. Trust me on that score.

I stretched, and that's when I realised that I wasn't wrapped up any more. It felt so good to stretch! I spent a long time stretching. When I rolled over, I saw her – my very own angel. Though, mind you, she didn't have no wings.

She was beautiful all the same, with long dark hair that hung in loose waves. Her eyes were green like oceans of grass. She wore a red dress that clasped at the shoulders with gold pins. Around both wrists were gold torcs set with emeralds. When she saw me awake, she smiled. I thought I was in love. Hell, I was in love. That woman was beautiful.

She had been standing at the entrance, which was a rectangular thing, trimmed in mud like the one and only window in this circular hut. A piece of painted hide served as the door. The woman had in her hand a tray with a bowl of rabbit stew on it.

Damn that smelled good. Let me tell you, soldier's rations are piss. This meal was bliss compared, and I was so hungry I barely waited for her to put the tray down before I dug in. I remember burning my tongue and her laughing at me. I loved the way her eyes crinkled at the edges when she smiled.

She waited patiently for me to finish eating before she collected the dishes and left. As she exited the hut, a man walked in. He looked like a Swede, to be honest, what with his height, and blond hair. He wasn't wearing a shirt, only hide trousers, and he was covered in tattoos. Angels with tattoos. Who would have guessed it?

He didn't seem quite so pleased with me as the woman was. He said something to me in a language I did not understand. It wasn't Swedish.

"What?" I asked. The man frowned, turned and left. I shrugged. Wasn't my fault I didn't speak their language.

Not sure what to do, I threw the blankets aside and stood. There was no way I was going to stay in bed, what with the sun shining like it was. It took me a moment to realise that I was naked. It was a warm breeze that alerted me to that fact. I looked down at myself. I was covered in scars, and the crinkled skin that covered my right side told me I had been burned pretty badly.

The man returned suddenly with clothes bundled in his arms. Well, a pair of trousers at any rate. He handed them to me with a grunt, then left again, just as surly as before. Maybe he was German.

In any case, I pulled the trousers on. They were a bit long for me, but otherwise fit quite well. Not knowing what to expect, I walked outside the hut and stopped short. There were just four other huts, and one great big rectangular one with stone steps that led up to massive wooden doors.

It was a small village, near as I could tell, made up of just five families. Well, six really, if you include the lucky bastards that got to live in the giant hall. Everyone had gathered at the entrance of the hut, no doubt them being told I was awake now, and all. They all just sort of stood there and stared. So I stood there and stared back.

One woman approached after a while. She sniffed me, then poked a strong finger into my rib.

"Ow!" I exclaimed. I pulled away, scowling at her with my best angry face. She turned to the crowd and giggled and then walked away. She left a bruise – a great big one – right on my ribs.

It was the pretty woman who broke up the staring contest. She clapped her hands sharply and said things in her bizarre language and, with a collective complaint, the crowd dissipated. The woman smiled and beckoned me to follow her. Ain't no way I was going to say no to this woman, no sir!

She showed me around this little village. It struck me then that there were no roads. There weren't any cars. Not even a bicycle. People walked everywhere, it seemed. And then I noticed the swords. Swords! I mean, some of the Limey officers carry swords, but they are small and decorative. The swords these villagers carried were huge things that were as wide as my neck.

I didn't understand. Clearly I hadn't died. I wasn't living on a cloud, no one had wings and there wasn't any harp music. This wasn't heaven. So what then? Had I gone back in time? I must have looked startled, because the woman placed her hand on my arm and looked at me with concern. I tried to smile, but I think it looked more like a crooked grimace.

We walked around the village a little more. It seemed everything was shared. There was a pigpen, and several cows that munched lazily on the grass and just watched the villagers bustle by in their work. Back behind the huge hall were three fields, one had hops and barley, one had wheat, or something that looked close enough to wheat, and the other was currently empty, though chickens were crawling over it like vermin.

That night, everyone went into the hall. I had a place of honour, or so it seemed, sitting beside the tall, surly blond man who, in turn, sat next to a massive older man wearing a brass crown. I kid you not when I tell you this man was huge. He wasn't fat. Every ounce of his mass was muscle and bone.

He could have crushed me with just a hug. The pretty woman sat on his other side.

The man wearing the crown tried to talk to me several times, but I had no idea what he was saying. He and the blond man exchanged a quiet word, and the king (what else would you call a man with a crown?) stopped trying. I ate really well that night, I remember.

They ate, and drank, and then drank, and then ate a little more, and spent the rest of the night drinking. I was tired by the end of it, and really glad when the king stood and left. The pretty woman escorted me to bed in my little hut, and then left.

The next day, I was dragged out of bed and hauled back into the hall by the blond man. He wasn't very gentle, and I thought I was in trouble. Once inside, I was faced by a woman dressed in a white robe and bent with age. She had striking blue eyes, and seemed to garner a lot of respect from everyone else. When she looked at me, it was as if she was looking into me. I tell you, it was unnerving.

The old woman said something to me.

"What?" I replied. She rolled her eyes and stepped forward, poking me between the eyes with a bony finger. These people liked to poke. She started talking again. This time her babbling slowly became comprehensible.

"Hello?" she was saying. "Hello? Is there anyone in there?"

I frowned. "How did you do that?" I asked, rubbing my forehead.

"Ah!" the woman said, clapping her hands together. "That's better. The savage can talk!"

"Savage? I'm not the one living in the Stone Age!"

The woman cocked her head in a strangely bird-like fashion, then shrugged. "What is your name?"

"Doug. Doug Sheen."

"Doug Sheen," the woman said with a yellow-toothed grin. "Why have you come to this village?"

I scowled. "I didn't!"

"Yes, you did," the blond man growled. "I was riding in when you jumped at me and knocked me off my horse."

"I did no such thing!" I insisted. "I was on the battlefield. Fighting a war. Then something exploded and I woke up here."

"Perhaps," the pretty woman said with a smile, "he was thrown onto your horse, husband."

Husband. Never been so disappointed in my life. The blond man grunted. "It is possible," he conceded.

"You wear strange clothes," the crone continued. "What kingdom are you from?"

"Kingdom? None. I don't live in a kingdom."

"That's absurd," the blond man snapped. "Everyone lives in a kingdom."

"Well I don't. We got rid of kings long ago. I'm from the U.S."

"Ewe-ess." the crone repeated, unsure.

"Yeah, the U.S. United States? On a huge continent. You should look it up."

"I have never heard of Ewe-ess," the crone said. "Is it in the north?"

"The... no. Well, maybe. Are we in Australia? I don't know where we are, so I can't tell you."

The crone grunted.

"He might be from the Otherside," the pretty woman said. The crone looked at her momentarily.

"I think you are right, he must be."

"The other side? I'm not the enemy!" I protested.

"No, no, you stupid man," the crone replied. "The *Otherside*. Don't you know anything?"

I had no idea what she was talking about. I stared blankly at her.

"Apparently not," the blond man grunted, and a few of the onlookers tittered. I glared. The crone sighed.

"We shall have to send you back."

I nodded. I had a war to fight, after all.

"The time is passed, however," the crone continued. "We shall have to wait until next year."

"Next year?" This could not be happening. Ain't no way I would let my friends be dying out there without me! "You have to take me back sooner!"

"We cannot. The divide opens only once a year, and you've missed it. We will wait until next year." She turned to walk away.

"Hey!" I shouted. "Hey! My friends are out there." I pointed in a random direction. "They need my help! You have to take me back!"

The crone turned back and opened her mouth to speak, but it was the pretty woman who spoke instead.

"Perhaps the wisps will take him."

The crone turned to her and cocked her head in thought. "Perhaps, but who will chance the journey to the Whispering Woods? I am too old to be fighting my way across the country."

The pretty woman looked expectantly at her husband who returned her gaze with a look that spoke defiance in volumes. Those sparkling green eyes of hers could not be resisted for long and the blond man sighed.

"Fine," he grumbled. "I will take him."

The crone shrugged nonchalantly. Of course she would. She didn't give a damn who I went with. I did. I didn't want to be stuck with Mr. No-Smile for the entire trip.

"Surely there must be someone else?" I asked. The crone raised her eyebrows at me.

"Don't be so quick to shun your guide. There is no one else you'd want at your side on a journey like this. Trust me."

What could I do? Squat, that's what. So I just sighed and muttered, "Fine."

The blond man grunted. "We leave tomorrow." He turned to leave.

"Can I at least have your name?" I asked him.

He turned back and replied, "Maddog."

It was all I could do to not laugh.

Maddog woke me up before dawn the following morning. "Dougsheen," he said, squishing my name together. "Dougsheen, time to awaken."

"Go away," I grumbled. "It's still dark."

"Best time to leave," Maddog replied with a grin. "Now, up."

I sighed and threw aside my blankets. I dressed in my trousers, and noticed that Maddog's usually exposed torso was covered in a chain mail shirt and a hard leather breastplate. He carried a bronze helmet under his arm and was armed to the teeth. Swords and knives of all sizes hung off every possible body part.

"Expecting trouble?" I asked.

Maddog only grunted. He pointed to where a set of similar armour was folded neatly, along with an array of weapons. Not a single gun among them. Let me tell you, for a soldier that only knows how to fire a gun, looking at a pile of swords and knives can be damned intimidating.

It was clear I knew nothing about anything to do with armour, and Maddog stared in utter disbelief as I tried to put it on.

"You really know nothing, Dougsheen," he growled before coming over to help me.

"We don't have this stuff where I'm from," I growled back.

"How do you fight without armour?" Maddog seemed genuinely puzzled at this. Puzzled enough to put aside his hostility for now at any rate. Thinking about it, it seemed odd that we were facing down guns and Lord knows what else without any protection other than the ability to fire back.

"We just do." It was all I could reply. Maddog grunted and shrugged. He helped me arrange the weapons, sighing with impatience the entire time. The dark night had given way to first light by the time he was done.

"We go now," he said grumpily.

I had thought we were going to ride out of the village, just like the heroes in those ridiculous faerie stories you hear. Not so. We left on foot.

"We aren't riding?" I asked as we left the village behind. Maddog shook his head.

"Horses are needed here."

It was just as well. I was a kid from New York; never ridden a horse in my life. For a long time we walked in silence. It was during this walk that I realised why we don't fight war with armour on. That stuff is bloody heavy! I challenge you to walk five steps in it, let alone miles and miles.

By the end of the day, I was exhausted. I collapsed onto the ground and stayed there while Maddog, rolling his eyes at me, prepared a fire. We ate salted pork and drank warm water for dinner. I fell asleep immediately afterwards.

It seemed too soon when Maddog was shaking me awake. It was still too early for the sun. I groaned but stumbled to my feet, staggering as I adjusted to the weight of the armour again. Maddog glared at me.

"Shut up," I grumbled. I heaved on my pack and we were off again, walking in stony silence.

"Soon we will come to the hungry grass. Be careful. It may swallow you, and there are biters."

"Biters? What the hell are biters?"

Maddog just smiled. We crested a small hill and found ourselves before a virtual ocean of tall grass that swayed like seaweed in the wind. I could hear the crisp zip of insect wings as they flitted in and out of the grass. Maddog made a face.

"Biters," he muttered in disgust. Then he turned to me. "Walk only where I walk."

"You're the boss."

I had to walk fast to keep up with his long-limbed strides. As we started wading through the grass, we kicked up a whole bunch of insects that buzzed angrily. At first I thought them relatively large wasps until one settled onto my mailed arm. It looked directly up at me with large, insectoid eyes. With a start I realised that what was settled on my arm, clinging to the mail with tiny hands and feet was, in fact, a woman - a bright orange woman with a set of four clear wings.

"Faeries!" I exclaimed. I went to pick her up. A mistake. She spun suddenly and sunk razor sharp teeth into my finger. It stung like fire. "Ow!" I roared, flinging the creature away.

Maddog started laughing, but his laughter turned into a roar of pain, as a faerie landed on his neck and bit down hard. I laughed, until I noticed that the faeries were starting to swarm.

"Run!" Maddog yelled. I didn't need to be told twice. We high-tailed it out of there, running hard for what felt like an hour before the faeries decided that we weren't worth the effort. "Must have had a nest there," Maddog said, rubbing the swollen bite on his neck.

I could only nod and pant as I tried to get my breath back.

"Come," Maddog said, slapping my shoulder hard enough to make me want to crumple. I grunted and Maddog and I walked through the field of tall grass until sunset, when we finally stumbled onto friendlier lawn. Maddog grinned at me.

"Rest now?"

I just grunted again and fell down to the ground, falling asleep instantly.

I woke of my own accord just moments after first light to find myself quite alone. My guide was nowhere to be seen. Realising I was starving, I pulled salted pork and bread from my pack and ate as I sat and waited for Maddog to arrive. It was just as the sun was rising that Maddog returned, with a grin on his face that turned his features suddenly boyish.

"Good, you're awake," he said. "Come, there is something you must see."

Frowning, I put on my pack and followed Maddog. We got to a hill and Maddog turned to me.

"Shhh," he hushed before crawling on all fours up the side of the hill. I followed, careful to make as little noise as possible. I tell you, it's bloody hard to be quiet when your shirt is made of metal.

Finally we reached the crest, and I peeked over. I could have choked. We were staring at a sizeable herd of horses. Only they weren't quite horses. They were unicorns.

I told you, you weren't going to believe me. What do you want? That's what I saw. They were unicorns, damn you. Only they weren't all white. Sure there were a couple of white ones, but like the mustangs back home, they came in all colours, the most common being brown. Maddog pointed to a big one, with a massive scar that ran down the length of its neck and down its chest.

"That is the stallion," Maddog whispered. "Has been for many seasons. But it is rutting season now, and he is getting old. Look, you see that one, the big black?"

"Yes?"

"He is the next contender. See how they are standing? There's going to be a fight!"

I know what you're thinking, because I thought the same thing. Unicorns are supposed to be all sweet and innocent and pure and some such nonsense, right? Well, I can tell you from first-hand knowledge, they ain't. These beasts are just as feral as wild horses, and it's damned frightening when they fight.

I watched in awe as the black one pawed the ground with a cracked hoof, then tossed his head and screamed. The big brown stallion tossed his head in reply. The black lowered his head so his dangerously sharp horn pointed at the stallion's chest and charged. I felt for sure that the stallion would be impaled, but he twisted to the side and brought his own horn down hard on the younger unicorn's horn with an almighty crack.

It dipped the black's head unexpectedly, and the beast stumbled. Over and over it went, each unicorn taking their turn to charge. It was ferocious and terrifying, and both beasts earned deep wounds that fight. They twisted and turned and pranced and screamed, coming dangerously close to the hill where Maddog and I were hiding.

"Too close," Maddog whispered. "Time to go."

We crawled back down the hill and jogged for a time. Behind me, I heard a piercing scream of victory. I never stopped to look back. I hope the stallion won.

When Maddog thought we were safe enough, we slowed down to a walk again. The unicorn sighting seemed to have loosened Maddog's tongue, and we talked for a while. I learned that Maddog was the son of a chieftain in a neighbouring village, and he had learnt all his battle-skills from a woman named Ava, who lived with her daughter on an island not far off the coast. He would be king one day, but it was the current king's daughter who would rule.

I told him that I knew people who fought for their king, and that his daughter would rule one day as well. I told him all about the war, and why we were fighting it.

"I hope it is as they say," I told him. "That this really is the war to end all wars."

Maddog sighed sadly. "There will always be war. People are stupid."

I laughed. He was probably right. "Still," I said. "I would like to try."

"You are a good person, Dougsheen," Maddog said after a long silence.

"You're not too bad yourself," I replied with a grin.

We walked all day every day for another week. At length we topped a steep hill and looked down over a valley. A small stream snaked its way through the valley. Behind the valley sat the borders of a forest.

"The Whispering Woods," Maddog said. "Come. Let us rest. We will go there tomorrow."

It was only midday, but I wasn't about to argue. It had been an odd week and a half. Over that time I had found that, despite his initial frostiness, Maddog was quite a humorous man and generous as well. I'd miss his company when I went home.

The next day, neither of us got up until the sun was well and truly in the sky.

"Now we go," Maddog said with a grimace after breakfast. I shrugged and stood.

"What will you do, when you go back?" Maddog asked as we trudged down the chalk slope. I shrugged.

"Go back to the fighting, assuming that the war didn't end already."

Maddog nodded. "That is good. Very brave. Many men do not return to war when they are healed."

"I understand that," I said. Truth be told, going back to the trenches was not my idea of fun, but I owed it to my friends, and all those poor sots that had been blown up before my very eyes. I had to go back.

"You could stay," Maddog offered. I smiled.

"Thanks, but I have to get back."

Maddog nodded. We walked in silence for the rest of the day. It was evening when we reached the forest's edge.

"Now what?" I asked.

"Now we wait."

"For what?"

"Wisps."

"What is a Wisp?"

"That," Maddog said. I turned to look and saw nothing but a small patch of fog floating quietly through the trees.

"That," I said, "is mist."

I should have known better than to not believe. Did I not see grassland filled with faeries? Had I not witnessed unicorns fight? The patch of mist probably heard me, and came flying forward, trees being no obstacle, to stop abruptly before us.

It remained as formless as any other patch of mist, but all the same, it looked at us with holes for eyes.

"Wisp of the wood," Maddog said, "Wanderer's Bane, this is Dougsheen, and he was blown here from the Otherside. There is a war there and he has left friends behind. He would return to them. Will you help him?"

It had never occurred to me before now that the wisps might yet refuse, and I would be stuck here for a year regardless. It was a tense moment as I waited. The answer was vague, nothing more than a sighing 'yes' on the breeze. Maddog nodded.

"Thank-you," he replied before turning to me. "Now listen carefully," he said. "Follow this wisp, and only this wisp. Ignore the lights. If you cross the path of another wisp, don't get mixed up. The woods have swallowed many a traveller, never to return."

I nodded. Maddog held out his hand, and I mine. He grasped my forearm. "Good luck, Dougsheen," he said.

"Thank-you Maddog."

I turned and, with a deep breath, followed the wisp, which had started to drift lazily back into the woods. Let me tell you, those woods were frightening. I could hear howling, and whispering. It was like I was being followed by invisible people who were talking to each other.

I remembered Maddog's advice well, and though the Wisp seemed intent on losing me in those woods, I never let it out of my sight. I walked all night until the woods seemed to thin out, and I could smell mud and smoke. The landscape changed suddenly. It was a battlefield, but one long ago abandoned. Grass and poppies covered the ground, ensnaring the barbed wire.

I looked around, realising I had lost the wisp. I turned to check the woods behind me, only to find that there were no woods behind me. I scowled.

I looked down at myself and noted that I was in my uniform. It had been washed and mended, but it was definitely mine.

The crisp crunching sound of many feet marching in time drew my attention and I looked up. I sighed with relief when I recognised the badges. 5th Battalion, British Marine Corps.

"Hey!" I shouted. "Hey! Guys!" I ran towards them.

"Identify yourself," the officer shouted at me.

"By God!" one of the marines said. "It's Sheen! Doug Sheen! Where the hell have you been?" That marine was Viktor Kusova, a friend of mine from the trenches. Not a bad Limey, but I reckon that was because his granddad was Russian.

"You'll never believe me," I replied.

"This is no time for jokes, mate. You've been M.I.A. for a year now!"

I stopped dead and my face fell. A year? It couldn't have been more than a month, recovery time included. All I could do was gape at Viktor in astonishment.

I was promptly arrested and escorted for debriefing. When I finished my tale, I was told I had delusions and was dismissed from service. Not that it mattered. A week later the war was over. Apparently we had won.

They put me in a home for crazy people. Friends came to visit, and asked after me, and asked what really happened. After a while, I stopped telling the truth. The truth always made my friends shake their heads sadly. I said I escaped from some prison or something. I said that there were no such things as faeries and unicorns, and nothing even remotely like a wisp. There certainly wasn't the 'Otherside' where people lived like it was the year zero.

After a year of lying my ass off, they let me go. I went back to the battlefield a few times, and just stood where I had been found by the 5th. It became a yearly pilgrimage. I saw a wisp once or twice, drifting across the battlefield, the Whispering Woods shimmering through its form as it drifted past.

All that happened some eighty years ago now, but I remember it clear as day. I'm too old now to travel, so I haven't been back there, but I bet there are wisps still floating around, ready to lead people into the woods if they can. You don't have to believe me if you don't want to. I don't care. The truth is, there is such a thing as magic, and all those faerie stories you heard as a kid, I'll bet my ass they're true.

You'll see.

The Undying

She was nobody. One of the many nobodies who lived their lives more or less as normally as possible. She wasn't very beautiful; pretty, but not beautiful. She was average height, average build, average intelligence. And now she was lying in a puddle of her own blood.

Her hand on the wooden Tiki she always wore, she stared out blankly at the back wall. The images of what happened before she was shot floating lazily through her mind as she struggled to breathe. A small smile touched her lips as she felt hands touch her shoulders and heard a familiar voice.

"Beth? Beth? Oh gods, Beth."

"I told you," she managed to wheeze. "You're not a true friend unless I'm willing to take a bullet for you."

Take one she did. Beth had stood in place of her friend and had been shot down.

They had been kept hostage for days. The university archery club, a small group of nobodies who happened to be at the wrong place at the wrong time, were taken captive when an angry atheist extremist group took over the gym.

Most everyone else managed to escape. The small indoor archery range had but one door, and thus, no exit for the club members when the group of angry anti-religion extremists charged through.

"We are here," one man said as he waved his gun frenetically at everyone present, "to free you all from the slavery that is religion – its outdated moral system, its need for unquestioning obedience, its corruption and thirst for blood. A world without religion – that is our cause. We are making this world safer for everyone."

"By holding people at gunpoint?" the coach demanded incredulously. He had been shot for that. A loud bang and a neat little hole appeared in his head. He fell backwards, stiff as a board. Some girls screamed.

Beth didn't.

All she managed was a gasp and a slow trickle of tears as the coach hit the ground. What followed was four days of terrifying hell. The leader of the heavily armed group would pace the floor and rant occasionally about the evils of religion. His hostages kept silent. The last person who pointed out his hypocrisy ended up shot in the head.

The gunmen set up radios so they could hear the news and communicate with the negotiators they were certain would try to talk them out. They would snicker to each other when the reporters would come on the air. Locked in that little room, radio was the only link to the outside world anyone had. Through it they learnt that the university had been evacuated and was, at that moment, surrounded by the army.

The negotiators were there on the first day. The demands that the captors made were untenable. They wanted every religious leader on campus to be brought to them for execution. The gunmen called them 'Shepherds of Hate.'

The hostages sat huddled together, weeping and pleading to no avail. Beth did not. She sat slightly apart from the group, dry-eyed and staring blankly at the far wall. Her mind was still. She was not afraid or angry, just sad.

Trouble had been brewing for years between outspoken atheists and equally outspoken believers. It started with bitter name-calling. The mudslinging became increasingly infused with threats of violence. Then, early last year, the atheist-run Centre For Progress was firebombed. In retaliation, they firebombed religious buildings of all kinds. Mosques, churches, monasteries, nothing was spared.

It became an ideological war of epic proportions. Extremists at both ends engaged in terrible acts of violence. Lynch mobs were common. Atheists would point to the violence as evidence of the evil of religion, even though they were guilty of exactly the same evil.

More moderate people from both sides of the debate would get together to try and create peace, recognising that hate, no matter the ideology behind it, was the ultimate evil. The extremists, however, remained criminally self-righteous, and they fought each other blindly. Now the battle had spilled over into the archery club.

On the fourth day of negotiations, the gunmen set their ultimatum. Either the religious leaders were brought forward, or they would shoot one of their hostages. For every day that passed with their demands unmet, they would shoot another hostage.

The first hostage they chose was Beth's friend, Lao. Lao was a quiet, gentle boy from Canton Province in China. He had come to study thermal dynamics, got involved in the archery club and found a kindred spirit in Beth. They quickly became good friends. It was a rare thing for Beth.

She had not had things easy in life, and her kind nature had been abused far too often for her to dare let anyone close. Beth was often accused of being cold by those who had met her.

Except Lao.

Lao was the one person besides her mother that Beth trusted at all and was thus showered with all the warmth and affection that was part of Beth's true nature. They were not lovers. All the same, Beth's love was strong. She would have done anything for Lao.

And so she did. When he was selected and pushed in front of the targets that hung at the far end of the room, it was Beth who fought the hardest to drag him back. When that did not work, she escaped the grasp of the armed man who held her fast and pushed Lao away from the target. He fell forward on his knees.

"You want to shoot someone," Beth yelled hotly. "Shoot me!"

"No!" Lao shouted. He rose to his feet and went to Beth. "Beth, what the hell are you doing?"

"I'm saving your life," Beth hissed back.

"You can't," Lao whispered. "You can't let them shoot you."

"I can't let them shoot you."

"Beth," Lao choked. He pulled her close in a tight embrace.

"You have to let me go, Lao," Beth whispered.

"No."

"Lao, they'll shoot both of us."

"Let them."

"No, Lao."

"I won't let them kill you," Lao whispered fiercely.

"Let me go."

"No." Lao was crying now, crushing Beth in a tight embrace.

"Lao."

"No."

Beth pressed her knuckle into the pressure point in Lao's armpit. It was not hard enough to kill him, but enough to render him unconscious for a few short minutes. Ironically, it was Lao who had shown it to Beth.

Lao slumped to the ground and Beth pushed him gently out of the way before standing upright again. She faced the executioner in silence. The leader of the militia and the executioner exchanged glances.

"Done your lover's tiff?" the leader said with a sneer.

Beth did not answer. She stood patiently in silence.

"Is there anything you'd like to say?"

The hostages all looked at Beth with wide eyes. Some were crying. Many in that small group had been training with her in the same room for three years, and not one, save Lao, knew her at all. Beth looked down at her unconscious friend, then back up at the executioner. She looked him directly in the eyes.

"I forgive you."

No one but Beth noticed the slight hesitation. Nevertheless, the masked man pulled the trigger on the rifle he had trained on Beth. It was not a clean shot. It struck her on her right side, piercing her lung. Someone screamed.

"Did you hear that?" the leader of the militia crowed into his walkie-talkie. "How many innocent lives do you think the so-called holy men are worth?"

Now Beth was lying on her side, the pool of blood spreading beneath her, and her lungs being slowly crushed by the escaping air.

"You're not my friend unless I'd take a bullet for you," Beth murmured.

"No, Beth," Lao cried. He rolled her over and lifted her head in his arms. Tears from Lao's eyes fell onto Beth's face.

"Don't cry," Beth soothed. She reached up and stroked Lao's face.

"You're not dead," Lao said. "So don't you go talking like you are. Any minute now, the army will storm in, and you'll be saved. Just keep breathing Beth. Keep breathing."

Beth smiled, and stopped breathing.

Lao sobbed quietly, pulling Beth close and rocking himself back and forth. He was violently torn from Beth's body as two of the militiamen hauled him away. Though he fought, grief made him weak and he was soon in the arms of his fellow archers.

The militiamen dragged Beth's body to the other side of the range, leaving a bloody streak in their wake. They laid her flat and covered her over with a black tarp, then sat and ate their evening meal.

"Hello Bethany," a deep masculine voice said from somewhere in the cavernous dark where she now lay. "Welcome home."

"Home?"

"Home."

"I don't understand. Who are you? Where are you?"

"Open your eyes, Bethany."

It was with some surprise that Beth understood her eyes were closed. She opened them and found herself in a room, on a bed, with fire crackling heartily in a nearby fireplace. There was nothing burning there, just the fire itself. Bethany sat up and looked about her. Sitting on plush chairs beside the fire was a tall man with dark hair and darker eyes. Beside him sat a woman with long waves of golden hair and pale blue eyes.

"We are the Lord Dark, and the Lady Light," the woman said. "We are the Undying."

Bethany blinked. Lord Dark rose to his feet. He was quite tall.

"You have made a sacrifice few others would, Bethany," he said in his deep voice. "For it, you have earned a place amongst us. You, like we, are the Undying."

"What does it mean, to be one of the Undying?"

"It means your soul is eternal," Lady Light replied. "And free now from corporeal form, you can move mountains."

"Move mountains."

"Yes."

Bethany frowned, then her eyes widened. "Lao!"

"Go, child," Lord Dark said with a smile. "Save your friends. We will wait for you."

The lights flickered as the militiamen were finishing their meal. They all looked up, then exchanged glances. Weapons at the ready, they took formation around the room and waited.

Lao did not notice. He knelt with the other hostages, his head bowed and his fist wrapped tightly around the jade Buddha he always wore around his neck. His prayers were for Bethany, that she find peace wherever she went now that this life was over for her.

Lao.

Lao's head snapped up and his eyes flew open. "Beth?"

Lao, listen to me. I need you to do something.

Lao looked about him. No one had spoken to him, though several people did cast him inquiring looks.

Lao! Concentrate.

"Where are you?"

It's a very long story, Lao. I'm going to cause trouble. The lights will go out. When they do, everyone will need to lie flat on the ground if they don't want to get shot. Do you understand me?

"Yes. Where are you?"

I'm everywhere, Lao. Beth's voice sounded irritated. Now spread the word.

Lao looked over at one girl, who was staring at him incredulously. "Cheryl," he whispered to her. "The lights are going to go out. When they do, lie flat on the ground, and lie still. Do not move. Spread the word."

Looking unconvinced, Cheryl nodded and did as Lao told her. It was not long before everyone had been told. Now everyone was casting strange looks at Lao. Lao did not care. He knew the sound of Bethany's voice anywhere, and he trusted it.

The flickering continued for a moment longer before all the lights blacked out. Clothes rustled quietly as the members of the archery club lay flat on their stomachs.

One lone light began to flicker again. It flashed light over the black tarp beneath which lay Beth's body. Beth's body was gone and the tarp had been casually tossed aside. The leader of the militia edged forward until he was standing on the tarp, stamping his foot over it in disbelief. The light continued to flicker.

"What the...?" another militiaman whispered.

The light went out.

Another light flickered and all eyes turned to it. It was the light at the end of the range, standing before the very target Bethany had been shot in front of. The lights flickered a moment longer, then went out. A shadow moved.

The militiamen sent a volley of bullets in the direction of the target, but struck nothing but the wall at the rear.

Sounds of a soft twang and three heavy thuds filled the dark room. Then three lights began to flicker, casting brief bursts of light over the bodies of three militiamen, each with an arrow sticking straight out of their foreheads.

"My God," one gunman breathed.

"Hey!" the leader barked. "None of that. This is just some army trick. That's all."

Lao.

"Yes?"

The door is open now. You will not be seen. Once down the hall, you can all get up and run.

"Run where?"

Out, Lao, you dolt!

"Right."

Spread the word.

It was slow going, but with Lao leading them, they slithered their way around the walls of the room. Lao was out first. He stayed by the door to ensure that everyone else got out safely. Then they were up and running. Behind them, sounds of gunfire and shouting filled the air.

The army pointed their guns at the escaping hostages as they approached.

"Identify yourselves!" one soldier barked. He had to scream as a news helicopter roared past.

"My name is Lao Kung," Lao replied, his hands held high. "We were all hostages in the university."

The soldier turned back. "Captain!"

A great deal of fuss was made over the escapees. Lao and the rest of the group were pushed through waves of rabid reporters into the back of an armoured bus and there they sat until the doors opened and a high-ranking army official walked in.

"We're a little surprised to see you," he said brusquely. "Which one is Lao Kung?"

"I am," Lao replied. Most everyone was still in shock. The thrill of freedom had not yet sunken in, cramped as they were in the bus. Lao was one of the more lucid members of the group.

"Tell me what happened."

Lao did, in detail, including the fight he had with Bethany over who was to die that day. He told the officer about the flickering lights, the arrows in the gunmen and the open door. He said he did not know who fired the arrows, thinking it a wiser recourse than asserting that someone had risen from the dead.

"That's quite a tale," the officer said, shaking his head.

"Sir," another soldier said from the door before Lao had a chance to retort. "The team's back. They said they're all dead. Every one. Arrows through them all."

The officer raised an eyebrow. "How poetic."

"Sir?"

"An archery club taken hostage, the captors all killed by arrows."

The soldier stared blankly at the officer. The latter sighed. "Never mind. The hostage that was killed?"

"A girl sir. They're bringing her body out now."

"What?" Lao demanded. He pushed past the officer and out of the bus. Two soldiers carried a stretcher made heavy by a body covered over with a black tarp. They set it down a few feet from Lao, who wandered over slowly. Kneeling beside the body, Lao pulled back the edges of the tarp.

Bethany lay on the stretcher, her face eerily white. Her eyes were closed and a small smile played about her lips. Lao's eyes filled with tears. He stroked her face.

"A pretty girl," the officer said gently, squatting beside Lao. "What was her name?"

"Beth," Lao whispered. The sound got caught in his throat and was uttered as little more than a squeak. He cleared his throat and tried again. "Bethany Shae."

"I'm sorry." The officer squeezed Lao's shoulder. All Lao could do was nod.

"Hey, check this out!" one soldier said to the other within earshot of Lao. "A wolf!"

"What's it doing in the middle of the city?"

"Here, I'll chase it away," the soldier said. He picked up at stone and lobbed it.

"You missed."

"Alright, you try, numb nuts."

The soldier never got the chance. Lao caught his wrist before the stone was thrown.

"Hey!" the soldier complained.

Lao didn't pay him any heed. There was something special about that wolf. Lao could feel it. He walked slowly forward, passed the hummers and reporters to the edge of the university campus. The wolf watched him approach with keen yellow eyes, quite unafraid.

"Sir?" the soldier called, hoisting his gun in case the wolf attacked. Lao still ignored him. He stopped a few feet from the wolf.

"Beth?"

The wolf cocked its head. Beth's voice, however, was decidedly absent. The wolf approached, lowered its snout to the ground and dropped something onto the grass. Looking at Lao once more, the wolf turned and trotted away. Lao bent down and picked up the object. A wooden Tiki pendant. He looked up to find the wolf looking back at him.

We are the Undying, a thousand voices said from everywhere all at once. *We are gone, but never cease.*

Then a single voice, one that Lao would recognise anywhere, spoke, *Farewell, Lao.*

"Goodbye, Beth," Lao whispered. "Thank-you."

The wolf vanished into the distance.

The Faerie Ring

What number
Used to dance and sing,
Betwixt the stones
Of the Faerie Ring?

What host
Would move and sway,
When night had
Taken over day?

Oh! To know
What they have known;
The many mysteries
Of that stone!

But it is forgot,
All too soon.
Yet, those stones remain,
Silent watchmen of the moon.

Her Father's Eyes

"What is it?" Rowena asked. The old-fashion key, rusted now with age, felt solid and heavy in her palm.

"It's a key, dear."

"Thank you, I figured that much out myself."

"The truth is I don't know what it's for. It's very old, though. My grandmother gave it to me on my sixteenth birthday, and she got it from her grandmother and so on down the line through Lord knows how many generations. I've tried it on every door on the property. It never worked. But it must be important. We never keep anything unless it's important."

"Right," Rowena drawled. "Uh, thanks, Grandma."

"You're welcome, dear; now run upstairs and finish your homework while I make your birthday dinner."

Rowena turned and bolted up the stairs to her room, slamming the door a good deal harder than she ought, and tossed the key on her dresser.

Most normal girls would be having a huge birthday party. They'd have mountains of presents, all of them cool; like an iPod or a diamond necklace.

Not Rowena, no. She had lived with her grandmother for as long as she could remember. Her mother had disappeared shortly after Rowena was born and Rowena had no idea where her mother and father were. There were no photos of either of them about the house.

As a result, Rowena had to spend her birthday doing homework and eating dinner with her grandmother, whose only gift was an old, useless, piece-of-junk key. Rowena kicked her school bag and sat heavily on her bed.

It wasn't her grandmother's fault. Old people are strange. Her grandmother was stranger than most and, according to Rowena's classmates at the all-girls grammar school she attended, so was she.

Rowena took up a brush and combed out her raven hair. She wasn't really sure what made her so different from everyone else at school, but she certainly felt different.

Sighing, Rowena set the brush aside and picked up her biology textbook.

She barely had time to open it when her grandmother called to her from the kitchen.

"Rowena! Dinner's ready!"

Rowena shut the book and thumped down the stairs. It smelled wonderful in the kitchen. Her grandmother had cooked lamb, her speciality and Rowena's favourite. They ate in silence. Rowena bit her lip and tried to stifle her hopes for more birthday gifts. Her grandmother seemed quite content to eat in silence. When dinner was done, Rowena bolted up the stairs again to start on her homework while her grandmother tidied up the kitchen, humming to herself.

Around ten o'clock, Rowena finally crawled between the sheets of her bed. There was a soft knock at the door.

"Yes?"

Her grandmother opened the door and bustled in with a tray laden with a jug of cold milk and honey and a small plate of biscuits. "Rowena, dear, would you like some milk and biscuits?"

Rowena sat up and smiled. "Yes, please."

"Here you are, love," Her grandmother said. She placed the tray on Rowena's lap and poured a glass of milk. "My mother used to give me milk and cookies before I went to bed every night and then sing me to sleep. I always had such lovely dreams after."

Rowena smiled at her grandmother. "Did you sing my mother to sleep?"

"Of course I did. That's what I'm here for," her grandmother replied. She reached out and stroked Rowena's straight hair wistfully. "You can tell that you are a Fae; all that straight black hair. You look just like her."

"Like who? Mother?"

Her grandmother nodded. Rowena bit back the question she had asked a thousand times over. There was no point in asking why her mother left her. Her grandmother never answered with anything but "I don't know, love."

Rowena finished her milk and biscuits. "Thank you."

"You're welcome, dear. Would you like anything else?"

Rowena shook her head, and her grandmother picked up the tray and started for the door.

"Actually..."

Her grandmother turned and raised her brows.

"Would you sing me to sleep?"

Her grandmother's smile could have lit the night sky. She put down the tray on the nightstand and sat beside Rowena, ensuring she was well wrapped in blankets and began to sing.

Hush, my love,
Sleep, my love.
Lady Night keeps watch,
Raiment of stars about her.
Hush. Sleep.

Hush, my love,
Sleep, my love.
Mistress Dream sings sweet,
Riding high upon the wind-horse.
Hush. Sleep.

Hush, my love,
Sleep, my love.
Lord Dark will not find thee,
For Lady Moon surrounds thee.
Hush. Sleep.

Her grandmother smiled gently and kissed Rowena's brow. "It never fails," she said, before picking up the tray and leaving Rowena to sleep. Rowena smiled to herself.

Rowena did not want to get out of bed. It took a great deal of her grandmother's cheerful cajoling to get Rowena to put her feet on the floor and get dressed. Her grandmother left to prepare breakfast. Late, as usual, Rowena threw on a pair of jeans and a crumpled shirt, chucked books haphazardly into her backpack, and wrenched open her bedroom door.

Rowena.

She turned to find the room empty and in its usual state. Nary a curtain rustled. Her gaze fell across the key that lay on her vanity top. She grabbed it before rushing out the door and down the stairs to the kitchen, putting the soft, breathy voice out of her mind.

"Rowena!" her grandmother greeted as she came through the kitchen door. Rowena grabbed the buttered toast from the plate her grandmother held and donned her red coat.

"I'm late." She dashed out the door.

"Have a good day, dear!" her grandmother called. If Rowena had heard, it didn't show. She grabbed her bike, a vintage thing so rusted it was likely to fall apart any moment, and jumped on.

It began to drizzle.

"Perfect. Just perfect," Rowena muttered darkly as she cycled up the hill.

Though one of the most prestigious schools in the town, she loathed almost everything about Cartier Girl's Grammar. Its posh façade, its ludicrous old-style buildings, built just twenty years ago, and the fact that all the teachers seemed to detest her. She especially hated her fellow students; perfect, pretentious blonde angels with their noses in the air, who turned into vicious harpies the moment a teacher's back was turned.

Rowena did love one thing about school, and that was her weekly forty-five minute music lessons. She was learning the lever harp and was certain that no instrument in the world could ever sound so beautiful.

Today was Thursday, and that meant two things; English class, which she despised, and her music lesson.

The rain grew steadily harder as the day wore on. Rowena stared out the window for almost every class and paid little attention to the teachers' lectures.

In English class, Ms. Rose droned on in an unwavering monotone about Shakespeare as Rowena's attention drifted outside once more.

"...has become the biggest problem. Rowena? Rowena, are you listening to me? Rowena Fae!"

Rowena snapped around. "It looks like there will be a storm this afternoon."

"What?"

"It...I'm sorry, Miss Rose, what were you saying?"

"Heavens, girl! You are the most difficult student I've ever had to deal with!"

Immediately following lunch, Mr. Westworth taught her music lessons. His gentle encouragement had made Rowena a fine harp player. Though elderly, he surely must have been very handsome in his youth, with eyes as green as spring grass—sparkling like dew in the morning sun—and a wide smile. He greeted her at the door of the music room with a towel, having spied her approaching in the pouring rain with nothing but her coat to shield her.

"Do you not own an umbrella, Miss Fae?" he asked her as she removed her coat and towelled off.

"I forgot it."

"Hmph. Make sure your hands are dry. I don't want these strings getting wet."

"Yes, Mr. Westworth."

Rowena sat at the harp, and Mr. Westworth opened the music book. "Right, what would you like to play?"

"Planxty Lady Wrixon."

Mr. Westworth smiled. "One of my favourites." He flipped the pages, and Rowena began to play. As always, she became lost in her music and did not notice a beautiful sound emanating from her coat pocket until Mr. Westworth shifted. She stopped, and the sound, like singing crystal, died away.

Frowning, Rowena rose from her seat and went to her coat. She fished out the ancient key. It did not look any different.

"What is that?" asked Mr. Westworth.

"A key. My grandmother gave it to me for my birthday yesterday."

"Well, Happy Birthday." He smiled warmly at her.

"Thanks."

"What's it for?"

"I don't know. Neither does Grandma."

"May I?" Mr. Westworth held out his hand and Rowena placed the key on it. He put it up to the light and examined it from all angles. "Well, it doesn't seem that special. Very old, yes, but not that special."

"It can't have been the thing that made that noise." Rowena frowned.

"Let's experiment, shall we?" Mr. Westworth placed the key on a side table and went to the harp. He began to play. Both he and Rowena watched the key carefully. It did nothing.

"Hmm." He sounded disappointed.

"Let me try."

Mr. Westworth gave her the seat and Rowena began to play. Not one bar into her Planxty, the key started to sing, the sound clear and high and sweet.

"Oh my!" Mr. Westworth breathed.

"I don't believe it!"

A rapid knock at the door brought them both back from their intense study of the key. "Mr. Westworth?"

Mr. Westworth snatched up the key as he called, "Just a minute." He pressed the key into Rowena's hand. "I do not know what this is for, but it's very special. Keep it close."

She nodded and hurriedly put on her coat. "Thank you, Mr. Westworth."

"No, no, my girl. Thank you."

With her mind awhirl, Rowena stepped out of the music room and ran to her next class in the pouring rain.

The rain did not let up for the rest of the day. By the time school ended, the thunder and lightning started. Rowena cursed savagely as she pedalled home in the downpour. The sky had grown dark, as if it were evening already. She arrived at the front door of her tiny house just as lightning struck immediately above and barged inside as the thunder shook the house.

"Heavens to Betsy!" her grandmother exclaimed as Rowena stumbled in. "You look like a drowned rat!"

"Thanks," Rowena mumbled.

"Come inside, child, and shut that door. I'll fetch you a towel."

Soaking wet and cold, Rowena did as she was bid. She shivered in the tiny foyer until her grandmother bustled back from the linen cupboard with an armload of towels.

"I only need one, Grandma." Rowena smiled gratefully nevertheless.

"That's what you think. You're still swimming. Now, off with your jacket and shoes."

Rowena removed her jacket, and her grandmother threw a towel around her shoulders. "Come on in, then. I'll run you a hot bath and make some tea. That should warm you up."

Rowena nodded and allowed her grandmother to fuss over her. It was not long until she found herself in the tub, surrounded by suds that smelled sweetly of strawberry and jasmine.

Her grandmother carried in a tray of chamomile tea.

"Here you are, love. Nothing soothes the body like a nice, hot cuppa." She poured the cup and handed it to Rowena, who took it and relaxed into the warm water. Despite the storm thrashing like a wounded dragon outside, inside this house, in the presence of her grandmother, Rowena felt safe and happy. How could her mother have wanted anything else? She lowered the cup from her lips without taking a sip.

"Grandma?"

"Yes, dear?"

"Why did mother leave me?"

"I don't know, love, but it was very wrong of her."

Rowena frowned. That was not the usual response. Her grandmother's tone sounded sharper than usual, angrier than the softly spoken, often sad responses of the past.

"What is it, dear?" her grandmother asked.

"Nothing." Rowena once again raised the teacup to her lips.

Don't! a strange voice shrieked from downstairs, ringing like crystal. Rowena's head snapped up, and she looked at her grandmother. "Did you hear that?"

"Hear what, love?"

"That voice."

"What voice, dear?"

"Nothing, never mind. Must've just been the house shaking. Do you mind if I just soak a bit?"

"Of course not, dear. Oh, silly me, hanging around in the washroom! Drink your tea and come downstairs when you're ready. I'll put some supper on the table."

"Thanks, Grandma."

Her grandmother left the bathroom, humming an unfamiliar tune. Rowena's scowl deepened.

"Hello?" she whispered to the empty air once her grandmother was out of sight. There was no response. "Rowena Fae, you have lost your mind," she scolded herself. She raised the cup once again.

No! came the shriek once more. *Run!*

"What?" Rowena whispered.

Run, Rowena! Run!

Gasping, Rowena jumped out of the tub, spilling her tea in the water. Her heart racing, she towelled off and ran into her room and threw on whatever clothes her hands touched.

Hearing her grandmother in the kitchen humming her strange song and clanging about noisily, Rowena crept as quietly as she could down the stairs to the door. She had only just reached for her coat when she heard her name. She turned and faced her grandmother, who stood at the kitchen doorway, draped in light, but looking dark.

"Where are you going, Rowena? You didn't drink your tea." The voice Rowena heard did not belong to her grandmother.

"I...I forgot something...at school," Rowena managed to stutter. "It's important. I have to go back and get it." She pulled her coat off the rack.

"No. You aren't going anywhere." Her grandmother drifted towards the door. Her toes dragged on the floor as she glided forward, her eyes blank and dark.

Rowena screamed. She turned, flung open the door, and raced out into the storm, coat in hand. She dared look over her shoulder only once, and through the haze of tears, she saw the lifeless form of her grandmother gliding after her, eyes boring into the back of her.

Running blind, Rowena mustered what strength she could and ran to the only place her feet knew where to go, Cartier Girl's Grammar.

Her grandmother, or what used to be her grandmother, still in pursuit, Rowena ran full long onto the campus. She rounded the corner of the Arts Building, and collided with something; something that let out a winded "harrumph" and spilled papers everywhere. Rowena screamed again as long, strong fingers wrapped around her arms.

"Rowena!" a familiar voice exclaimed.

Rowena looked up into the sparkling green eyes of Mr. Westworth.

"Mr. Westworth!"

"Rowena, whatever is the matter?"

"Let me go please, sir," she begged, struggling against his strong grip.

"Come now. Let's get out of this storm and you can tell me all about what's going on."

Mr. Westworth gently pulled Rowena around the corner she had just rounded, despite her protests. He stopped dead when he saw what she had been fleeing from. Rowena's grandmother hovered inches from the ground before him. She looked older, dried-out and brown, and wearing a tattered white dress. Her eye sockets were empty, as if worms had eaten her eyes long ago. Even still, they seemed to glare at the pair standing before her.

"Grandma!" Rowena squeaked.

The old woman peeled back her lips in a snarl, exposing yellow, sharply pointed teeth.

Mr. Westworth pulled Rowena behind him. The woman struck him hard with clawed hands, scratching his cheek and drawing blood from four parallel cuts. Rowena screamed. With a desperate kick, Mr. Westworth sent the phantom flying backwards. He spun about and pulled Rowena back around the corner at a dead run. "Run!"

Sobbing and clutching his hand, Rowena ran.

"Where are we going?" she yelled through the storm.

"I have an idea."

They ran out of the school grounds and passed the dilapidated shed that marked the border of a neighbouring sheep farm.

"What the...?" Rowena asked incredulously as Mr. Westworth picked her up and helped her over the low stone wall bordering the sheep's paddock. Unperturbed by the intruders, the sheep stared and chewed on the soaking grass.

"Go!"

"Go where?"

"Straight! Run straight!"

Rowena's legs pounded the earth. Mr. Westworth soon caught up with her. He grasped her hand again, and they ran to a large, fenced-off square in the centre of which stood a small stone circle. They reached the edge of the circle and Mr. Westworth grabbed her shoulders.

"Do you have the key?" he asked.

"What? Why?"

"Just answer me! Do you have it?"

Rowena fumbled in her coat pockets and, for a moment, feared she left it behind. Relief flooded through Rowena when her fingers curled around the metal and she pulled the key out.

"I once saw your mother use a key like that."

Rowena looked up at him in surprise.

"It was a long time ago. I was just a young lad, no more than seventeen. I thought it had been a dream. Time does not move the same in her world. I thought she was just a dream. Rowena Fae..."

"What is it?" Rowena asked. Mr. Westworth's expression clouded as he struggled with himself a moment. Then his face set in resolve.

"I'm sending you home." He pushed her roughly into the circle. "I dare not go further. Hold onto that key, Rowena, and sing."

"What?"

"Sing, Rowena! Sing!"

Sighting the phantom gliding over the paddock, sending the sheep into a frenzied panic as it did so, Rowena opened her mouth and tried to sing. Her throat was so dry that no sound came from it at first. Rowena looked into Mr. Westworth's kind eyes. He smiled at her and Rowena found her voice again. It was shaky at first but grew stronger as the song began to take shape. Planxty Lady Wrixon, her favourite tune.

Rowena watched in surprise as the stones of the circle began to glow. Faintly at first, and then it became a warm, honey colour as the key began its crystalline singing in response to Rowena's own music.

"Give my love to your mother," he called as the glowing intensified.

The phantom woman reached the edge of the stone circle. Rowena watched helplessly as Mr. Westworth turned to face her, his hands raised in defence.

The phantom raised one clawed hand high and brought it down hard on his head.

Rowena screamed. She never saw him hit the ground. The bright glow flared, blinding her.

When she could see again, she found herself in the stone circle, but the fence had vanished. In place of stone walls and sheep, open grassland, greener than she could ever have imagined, rolled in gentle waves to the horizon. The sun shone brightly and birds sang as they flew overhead.

After a few minutes, she noticed a young woman, dressed in a long, flowing red dress tied at the shoulders with ornate gold clasps standing on the edge of the circle. Rowena stared at her. She was the most beautiful thing Rowena had ever seen. It took her a moment longer to realize she recognized the woman standing before her.

"Mother?"

The woman smiled and opened her arms to Rowena. Rowena stumbled forward, fear and relief making her legs next to useless, and sank gratefully into the woman's embrace.

"Oh, my child," the woman said. She laughed through her tears. "It's alright now. You are home now. You are safe."

"What happened? To me? To Grandma?"

"It was Samhain when you stumbled into the circle," Rowena's mother said. "And it was too late when we realized what had happened. You were but four years old then and had no way to return. We sent Doris through to look after you until you were old enough to...to come home."

"Doris?"

"You called her 'Grandma.'"

Rowena's eyes filled with tears as she remembered the kindly old woman who had looked after her since she could remember, and the terrible phantom that had masqueraded as her.

"What happened to her?"

"The Fir Bolg have long used dark magic to hunt us. Poor Doris. Her sacrifice was greater than any we could have imagined."

"Why didn't she tell me?"

"Sweet child, no one is allowed into the Land of the Sidhe unless they can prove themselves pure of heart. It was a secret that had to be kept until you were ready to know; to preserve your innocence, or you would never have been able to come back. And this land needs its princess. Oh," her mother sobbed, "look how beautiful you've become." She pulled Rowena close once more. "I have missed you so."

Rowena pulled back and smiled up at her mother. Her mother's raven black hair fell straight to her shoulders, but her eyes were a startling blue.

"You look just like I did at your age," Rowena's mother said, as if guessing Rowena's thoughts. "But for your eyes. Green as spring grass, and sparkling like dew in the morning sun. You have your father's eyes."

Lady of Shadow

Scatha remembered when the Crimson Guard had come. There had been warnings from family across the channel that the crazed leader of the guard had his eye on the sacred isle.

He had tried once before, but the island had ideas of her own, and his boats were shattered against her cliffs in a violent storm. There is only so much an island can do, however. The second attempt saw the guard get through with only one third of their ships smashed.

The Crimson Guard marched through the island, burning the villages of the chieftains that refused to capitulate, raping the women, and slaying all the men and children. They said they were cleansing the island of the impure savages.

It was not the islanders who plundered their own lands into desolation. It was not the islanders who marched, pillaging and raping in a desperate bid for resources. The islanders weren't the savages. The Crimson Guard were; savages in crimson silk.

Scatha hated them.

Scatha's father had been a low-level landholder. He had only nine men in his employ and just three tenants who farmed his fields. They were as family to him, he told Scatha and her brother, Brandon. He was their father, and it was his responsibility to protect them. In turn, like dutiful children, it was their charge to aid and look after their father.

"Never," her father warned his children one evening, "take that care for granted, and never expect it unless you are willing to do your utmost to return the duty."

The tenants loved Scatha's father. They would greet him with smiles and waves as he inspected their farms. He would sit and talk with them awhile, discussing mundane things like the rain or whatever insect was most rampant and other such things that farmers were wont to talk about.

Every feast day was observed. Scatha's father held his hall proudly, and served the farmers himself. They loved him for that most of all. It was no surprise, then, that the farmers stayed and fought for him when the Crimson Guard attacked.

That night was terrible. Scatha's father had set a watch when he heard the news that the Brignoves were attacked. Not three nights later, the warning horn blew. Scatha's father had planned it well. The farmer's wives and children were to gather in the woods while the fighting was going on.

Brandon and Scatha were to go with the wives and children. Brandon put up a great fuss, as did Scatha. They weren't about to let their father face the Crimson Guard without help.

Farmer's wives, however, are very strong. The two children weren't given a choice, and were hoisted off the ground and hauled out of the hall. Brandon stopped his shouting only when one of the wives told him to hush, or be the cause of a sword in her belly. They were partway to the forest when everything flared orange.

Scatha looked back. Everything was on fire; the farmhouses, the pens with the cattle and pigs panicked inside, and the hall. Her mother and father were in the hall still. Scatha screamed, and Brandon turned.

Brandon was much like his father; brave and foolhardy. With an angry shout, he twisted out of his caretaker's grasp. In an instant he was down the hill. Scatha watched in horror as he tried to pick up a sword twice his height, and was run through by a member of the Crimson Guard.

Scatha screamed and escaped her own guardian. She didn't try to pick up a sword when she reached the bottom of the hill. Instead, she charged at one of the Crimson Guard and, yelling and cursing with all the foul words an eight-year-old could know, she punched and kicked ineffectually at his steel plating.

The man laughed, pushed her back so hard she fell down, and unsheathed his sword.

"Stupid little savage," he spat as he raised his sword high.

"Stop!" another one called. "That one's a girl. She might be worth something."

The man standing above Scatha looked upset at being denied his kill, but he obeyed with a barely heard grumble. Another guardsman picked her up by her hair. She screamed and kicked while he laughed.

"Feisty, this one," he noted. "Would make a fine whore."

"Put it away," the one who had saved Scatha's life said wearily. "She'll not be touched. They aren't worth half as much broke, and you know it."

The guard's face fell and Scatha kicked him in the chest. In retaliation, he shook her by her hair and threw her into the mud. The men laughed and she was hauled onto her feet. They bound her wrists with chains wrapped so tightly that her fingertips went numb. Her feet they left unbound. Scatha had to march with them, they said.

It was two days of solid walking. Scatha tried to escape three times. The leader of the guard got so frustrated that he bound her feet and hauled her over one shoulder. He was neither as tall nor as broad as Scatha's father, so it was an easy thing for her to squirm her way off his shoulder.

That's when the cruel man who had pulled her hair hit her over the back of the head with a rock. The world went black.

Scatha woke up next delirious and nauseous. She saw a pale face next to hers that, though grimy, looked like an islander.

"Where are we?" she whispered to the boy.

"We're on a boat," he answered dully. "They're taking us to the slavers in the desert."

Scatha quailed. She had heard of the desert only once. Her father described the people there as the cruellest men in the world. The thick, cloying perfumes they wore could not hide the stench of evil that surrounded them.

Scatha wanted to cry. Instead, she took a deep, shaky breath. "Stay strong," she told herself. "Remember mother's example."

Scatha's mother was the most elegant woman she knew. The Lady Hafwen always carried herself proudly. Even surrounded by women with more jewels, she always seemed radiant.

"I have it better than all those women," Scatha remembered her saying. "For I married a good man, whom I love very much. Be wary, my sweet. Do not be fooled by riches. Gold is cold, and the men who possess much of it are infected with its chill."

Even in the reeking bowels of a leaky ship, Scatha smiled at the memory of her mother's words. Then, wearied by exhaustion and the dull aching in her head, she slept.

The captives were all rudely woken by a sharp jerk on their chains. Scatha's arms almost came out of their sockets. She groaned and sat up, her head spinning wildly. It was only then that she noticed she was hungry.

"Up!" a guardsman demanded. "Get up! Up!"

Scatha struggled to her feet and followed the procession of chained captives out of the hold. The sunlight struck her eyes so fiercely as to be blinding. She tried to cover her eyes, but her hands were chained to her feet and she could not lift them. She squinted as much as she could without actually closing her eyes.

When at last her eyes adjusted, what she saw took her breath away. There was no greenery. There was only blinding white sand.

A sea of tents blossomed at the end of the docks. The tents themselves were nothing more than brightly coloured cloths tied to four tall pillars with stabilising ropes staked into the ground.

Under the pavilions sat hundreds of people, all of them chained. Most of the men in chains had skin as dark as ebony. It shocked Scatha.

"Get a move on!" a guardsman roared, lashing out with his whip on the back of the foremost person. Scatha winced as she saw the skin split and blood spill down his filthy back.

As one, the new slaves all shuffled forward. Scatha glanced behind her to see the boy she had spoken to on the boat. He was dreadfully skinny, and his grey eyes were dull and lifeless. She smiled at him, but received nothing in return.

The chain of slaves was stopped at the end of the docks. There, one of the Crimson Guard met up with a man dressed in many layers of flowing cloth. Even his head was covered. Scatha thought he must be dreadfully hot. They shared a brief conversation in a language she did not understand, then the slaves were all forced to turn into a line as the strange man with nut-brown skin inspected them.

"They're too skinny!" the strange man said, his accent so thick Scatha could barely understand. "Skinny slaves don't sell – especially the girls. Girls should be plump, plump and delectable." He looked directly at Scatha as he spoke. She shuddered.

"Well, they all made it through alive. You know livestock always loses weight during shipping. You can fatten up the girls to your heart's desire once they're yours."

"Come into my tent. We will discuss these rabid skeletons."

The two men disappeared and the new slaves were ushered beneath a pavilion to wait. One girl far down the line began to cry. Scatha wanted to, but wouldn't. Her father would have been ashamed to see her weep.

"Stay strong," she whispered to herself. "Stay strong."

The guardsman and the slaver spent all day haggling over price. The slaves themselves one by one succumbed to exhaustion, or despair, or both, and sank to their knees. Many were crying. Scatha stared blankly out of the pavilion, ignoring everything and everyone around her.

Before the sun went down that day, the nut-brown man in too many clothes returned.

He spoke to the soldiers all in black that stood at the four corners of the pavilion in his bizarre language. One soldier nodded and walked away. Another one proceeded to replace the single chain with individual shackles for each slave. When the soldier unlocked Scatha's shackles, Scatha caught sight of a Crimson Guardsman she recognised. He was stumbling in the hot evening air, leering at the slave girls as he went.

All else faded to white. Scatha surprised the soldier with an angry roar. She broke the line and charged at the guardsman. With another angry yell, she pushed him so hard it would have floored a sober man.

"Coward!" Scatha screamed, throwing herself on top of him and raining punches on his face as hard as she could. "Coward! Bloody savage!"

Strong arms wrapped around Scatha's waist and hauled her off the guardsman. Scatha twisted, throwing a sharp elbow into the nose of a soldier. The man dropped her and stumbled backwards, clutching at his nose. Another soldier approached, drawing a dagger from his belt.

Scatha stood her ground, her hands balled into bloodied fists. The man was almost upon her when he was grabbed from behind. An ebony-skinned slave wrapped long limbs around the man's shoulders and used the chain to crush his throat.

"Run, little girl!" the ebony slave yelled in a deep voice with a strange accent. "Run!"

A blade from behind the slave struck down, point first, into the slave's shoulder, and he fell to the ground with a grunt. Scatha turned and ran. In a camp filled with slavers and soldiers, she did not get far. She was dragged back to her new owner by her hair, kicking and screaming all the way.

"Unseemly," the slaver who now owned Scatha said with a shake of his head, "for a girl to act so in this way. In my land, that is not allowed."

"I hate you!" Scatha hissed at him.

"A little cat are you?"

Scatha lashed out with her feet, but did not manage to kick the slaver. "I hate you! I hate you!"

The slaver grunted, stood, and walked away. "Scrub her down. I believe I have a buyer for this one."

Scatha was dragged away once more. She was shackled, though she gave the soldier a few bruises in the process. In retaliation, the soldier slapped her hard across her cheek. She was then tied to a post and her clothes torn from her.

Hot water rained upon Scatha and she was scrubbed down with a stiff-bristled brush until her skin was pink. She screamed and shouted until she had no voice or energy left to shout with. Cleaned and towelled off, Scatha was given a loincloth to wear and a small wrapping for across her chest, and that was all.

In this heat, Scatha was almost glad. She returned to the pavilion to find that most of the other slaves had also been washed and changed into similar attire. All the girls had the strip of fabric across their chests. The boys and men had their chests left bare.

Scatha was tied to a post at the edge of the pavilion and left there. Still seething, Scatha scanned the crowds in the pavilions around her. She caught her breath when she noticed one ebony-skinned slave sitting against a pole and struggling to breathe. From the base of his neck gushed blood.

"He does not have long to live," the soldier standing over Scatha told her in his thick accent. "It was foolish of him to help you."

Scatha's eyes filled with tears as the slave's fluttered open. The tall, muscular man smiled at Scatha and she did her best to smile back.

"Will you take me over to him?" Scatha asked the soldier quietly. The man looked at her in surprise.

"No."

"Then please, bring him to me, that I might thank him."

"No."

"Please." Scatha's eye brimmed over with tears, though she tried hard to stop them.

"No."

Scatha broke down sobbing and did not look up until a shadow obscured the evening light. She looked up to find the slave swaying dangerously before her. He fell to his knees and smiled weakly.

"So they caught you after all, little Lioness."

Scatha nodded. "I could not run fast enough."

"Ah, you are young yet. You will learn to run."

"Thank you," Scatha replied. "For helping me."

"You are brave," he whispered. "And I would not be a man if I did not help."

"Come," Scatha said as gently as her sobs would allow. "Lay down and let me cool your brow."

The man smiled and lay down, his head resting on Scatha's lap. Scatha stroked his brow and blew gently across it, easing the fevered heat that had settled there.

"You are pretty," the man said. "For a ghost-skin."

Scatha laughed a little, but the laughter turned to wracking sobs when the light faded from the slave's eyes and his weight slumped. She bent down and kissed the man's smooth brow.

"That's enough, now," the soldier said gently. He turned and shouted some orders, and men in white robes and headdress that obscured all but the eyes came shortly thereafter, carrying a stretcher.

"No," Scatha cried as they lifted the dead man from her. "No."

"Down now," the soldier said, pushing Scatha back down. "He's dead. There's nothing you can do."

Scatha knew he was right. She watched listlessly as they carried the body of the dead slave away.

"He was a hunter of the Mubou people. They are very proud, and very brave," the soldier said.

"He was very brave," Scatha echoed.

"He respected you a great deal. The Mubou kneel before no one."

Scatha felt fresh tears sting her face. "He died for nothing. I could not escape."

The soldier grunted, but said no more and Scatha's green eyes continued to overflow.

Scatha did not know when she fell asleep. She had been weeping to herself one moment, and the next, she was being shaken awake by the soldier.

"This is the one?" she heard an accented voice say. She looked up and saw the slaver from the day before and a new nut-brown man dressed in robes and headdress. The man was handsome, with strong features and a black beard that was trimmed neatly.

"That is her. I hear a Mubou hunter named her 'Lioness'."

"A Mubou hunter? Truly?"

"I do not deceive."

"Hm."

The slaver gave a signal and the soldier hauled Scatha to her feet. The new man inspected her.

"She is scrawny."

"Pushed over a Crimson Guard."

"He was drunk. A flea could've done it."

Scatha resented that. "Only girls wear dresses," she spat hotly.

The handsome man's face cracked into a wide smile. Then he struck her hard on her cheek, giving her a matching bruise to the one the soldier had left. Scatha stumbled, but did not fall. She turned her head slowly to glare at the man.

"Worse awaits a mouthy slave of mine. I'll have you flayed alive, little girl."

"And they call us savages," Scatha answered. The man laughed.

"How much do you want for the runt?" he asked the slaver.

"Come into my tent," the slaver replied. "We will talk."

Scatha sat and sulked while the men talked.

It was well and truly past midday when they returned. The slaver said something to his soldier in the language Scatha did not understand, and she was untied from the pillar. She stared in anger as her chains were handed over to the new man.

"Come, girl," he said, tugging her chains. "Come."

Scatha yanked back so hard it dragged the man back half a step. In return he pulled out a riding crop and beat her side three times with it, hard enough to draw blood.

"Little bitch!" he snapped every time he struck. Scatha bit her tongue to stop herself from crying out and when it was done, she straightened and stared at him in the eye.

"Don't you worry, you stupid little barbarian," the man said. "The fighting cages will take away that pride of yours."

"You don't know the women of the Isle," Scatha replied. She hoped it was true. The Crimson Guard spoke of island women with morbid reverence. She hoped to live up to that reputation.

"Oh, but you are just a little girl, and you can be moulded into any form I wish."

Scatha scoffed at that, but said no more. She was walked back down to the docks, and shoved on another boat. She noticed that she was not the only other slave the man had purchased. Most of the others were men, some boys, and one or two women. Many of the men wore ebony skin and were well muscled, and quite tall. All of them stared at her with flat, unimpressed eyes.

It was not long before the boat began to creak and sway, and Scatha knew that she was sailing once more. She looked about her in the dim light. No one was looking at her.

"I am Scatha," she said.

One ebony-skinned man looked up. He was young, not much older than fourteen.

"We do not talk to each other," he said. "And we do not tell each other our names." The boy's accent was musical, and familiar.

"Are you Mubou?" Scatha asked. The boy turned to her with a frown.

"How does a ghost-skin know of the Mubou?"

"A Mubou man tried to help me escape. He called me Lioness."

The boy looked at Scatha strangely, but said no more.

"What is your name?" Scatha asked. The boy couldn't help but smile.

"Are all ghost-skins as annoying as you?"

"I imagine so, though Brandon would say I'm extra annoying." Scatha swallowed back tears as she said Brandon's name.

"Was he your husband?"

"Brother."

The Mubou hunter was silent for a while. "I am Jemmi," he said at length.

Scatha smiled at him, but could not bring herself to speak more. Memory of her brother had made her throat tight and tears stream down her cheeks.

"Do not cry, little Lioness," Jemmi said. "With luck we will all be dead soon."

Jemmi put one long arm around Scatha's shoulders and Scatha leant into him.

"Where are we going?" Scatha asked when her tears had stopped flowing.

"To the fighting cages," Jemmi replied. "But you are a girl and will not be made to fight. You might be going to the Master's bedchamber, or perhaps given to one of his sons."

Scatha shuddered. "He is not my Master. And I'd rather fight."

Jemmi laughed. "Then fight, little Lioness. Fight for your life."

It was a week of sailing, then two days more by caravan before they arrived at their destination. In that time, Scatha and Jemmi had become friends. Jemmi had his arms wrapped protectively around her when they dismounted the camel-drawn cage. Those arms were ripped away when the slaves were separated by gender. Scatha struggled as she was dragged away. Jemmi did nothing but watch her go sadly before he was ushered into the pits that held the fighters.

Scatha herself was dragged into the whitewashed house and made to stand with the rest of the frightened girls. Many were crying. One was so frightened she wet herself. Closing her eyes and taking a deep breath, Scatha forced herself to be calm. When she opened her eyes, she found the handsome man looking directly at her. She narrowed her eyes at him and he laughed.

"Perhaps in time, if you are good to me, you might learn to like me some."

"I'd rather die in the cages," Scatha spat.

The man laughed. "I will knock the spirit out of you."

"I am a woman of the Isle," Scatha replied.

The man laughed again, then struck Scatha across her calves with his riding crop. Scatha gasped in pain and fell to her knees.

"There will be worse to come if you don't behave yourself."

Scatha gritted her teeth and stood, defiantly returning the man's gaze. The man laughed again, then struck Scatha across the side of the head. The world went black.

When Scatha next woke, scantily clad girls were attending her. She groaned.

"Oh!" one girl gasped. "You're awake."

Scatha turned her head to look at the girl.

"You really shouldn't have challenged the master like that," the girl said, applying more wet bandages to her head.

"He's not my master."

"You've been sold."

"I was stolen."

"It is the same."

"It's not the same!"

The girl sighed and continued to apply the bandages. "If you do as he says, he's not a bad master," the girl said after a long silence. Scatha gritted her teeth.

"I'd rather die in the cages."

"Don't say that, or he'll throw you in there and then you'll be sorry."

"Let him."

So it was that Scatha lived in the whitewashed house as a slave. When the food came, she forced herself to eat. She had to stay strong in order to fight, and fight she would.

Scatha was not above doing everyday chores, and so did them with little fuss. It was when she had been summoned to the bedchamber that there was trouble.

"You seem to be settling in well," the man said, pouring two glasses of strong summer wine.

Scatha scowled at him and said nothing.

"Here," the man said, handing her a cup of wine. "It helps for the first time."

Scatha took the cup, sniffed its contents, then, keeping her eyes on the man before her, she emptied it onto the tiled floor. The man slowly placed his glass down on a nearby table and stared at the girl, his face turning bright red just as slowly.

Scatha let the goblet fall from her hands, and the man lost his temper.

"You vile, ungrateful wretch!" he roared, rushing forward. Scatha danced away from his grasp, knocking into another table as she did so.

"Come here and do your duty!"

"I'd rather die in the fighting cages!"

"Come here!"

"Stay away from me, or you'll regret it!"

"I am your master!"

"You are not my master! I have no master! I am a lady of the Isle!"

"I'll boil you alive!" the man roared.

Scatha screamed involuntarily as the man finally managed to catch her. He wrapped his arms around her waist and threw her bodily against a wall, his weight pinning her there.

"Let me go!" Scatha screamed as she squirmed. With nothing else available to her, she bit down hard, her teeth cutting through flesh and drawing blood. The man roared and threw Scatha away from him. She crashed hard against the table holding the wine decanter. Glass shattered as Scatha tumbled over, cutting into her side in several places.

The man staggered forward and picked Scatha up by her hair. "Rather die in the fighting pits, would you?" he hissed in her ear. "Fine. Your wish is granted!"

Dragging her by her hair, the man hauled Scatha out of the house and into the pits where the fighters were kept.

The sudden appearance of the master and his soldiers created a buzz amongst the fighters. The buzz became a roar when the fighters noted a girl being dragged in. The girl was tied to a post in the middle of the den. Jemmi tensed when he realised that the girl was Scatha.

"Little Lioness," he said in his lilting Mubou accent. "Look at me. Look only at me."

Scatha nodded, though her eyes were wide and frightened. She stared at Jemmi as the first of the lashes hit her back, and again at the second. Then her eyes lost focus and she slumped.

The master lashed her twice more before shaking her hard on the shoulder to wake her. Scatha's head lolled, but her eyes opened.

"This girl," the master said, "has defied me! She said she would rather die in the fighting pits than do her duty. So I'm granting her wish. Boys, she is all yours."

Scatha stifled a sob as an excited hiss ran through the mob and tens of pairs of eyes fell on Scatha. The master turned and left, sparing not even a glance for the girl tied to the post. Jemmi stood.

"This is my woman," he declared. "No one touches her but me."

There was an angry murmur.

"You want to fight me? Do you? Me, a Mubou hunter? Come up then, come up and try to steal my woman."

"You cannot fight all of us," someone yelled.

Jemmi swore in Mubou. "Can't I? Come see."

No one moved.

"You see, you all know what a Mubou hunter can do. Now go away. I want my woman in peace."

The crowd slowly dispersed, some more keen to avoid the hunter's rage than others. Jemmi turned and cut Scatha loose.

"Thank you," Scatha murmured from her crumpled position on the dusty ground.

"Do not thank me yet, little Lioness. These men are hungry. They will try to take you."

"Better them than him."

"Do not say that."

Jemmi picked Scatha up gently and carried her to his private cell. He laid Scatha gently on her side and examined her back a moment.

"I cannot treat this on my own. The doctor must come."

Scatha did not answer, she lay on her side and trembled, fighting tears.

"Hush, little Lioness. Stay strong."

At those words Scatha turned. She reached out and touched Jemmi's face. "Thank you, Jemmi," she whispered before her hand fell and she lost consciousness. Jemmi sighed.

The doctor came the next day and it was another two days before Scatha got off the plank that served as a bed. Jemmi was immediately at her side.

"You should be resting, little Lioness."

"It's alright, Jemmi," Scatha answered. "I must be strong."

Jemmi sighed. "I am to fight next week. I am matched against a very big man. You need to learn how to defend yourself in case I do not return."

Scatha's eyes grew wide. "But you have to come back!"

Jemmi smiled sadly. "The Mubou are feared because we fight lions. But sometimes, little Lioness, the lion wins."

Scatha wanted to cry again, but instead she closed her mouth and nodded. "I will need to learn to defend myself," she whispered. Jemmi smiled.

"You are brave."

Scatha tried to smile at him, but it didn't quite work.

Training began the very next day. It was slow at first, but Scatha learnt very quickly, and she was fast. A week later, Jemmi was gone.

Scatha paced his cell waiting for news. At dusk, he returned bringing with him a bounty of food.

"The hunter defeated the lion," the tall Mubou said with a broad smile.

"Jemmi!" Scatha shrieked in delight. That night, they ate very well and Scatha and Jemmi exchanged stories of their homes. It was this way for many nights, and many years.

In that time, Scatha had grown into a beautiful young woman, if a little skinny, and a very good fighter. She had won the respect of the fighters in the den, and had fought many times in the cages. Jemmi, a hunter of a tribe renowned for their self-control, was starting to get tense.

"What is wrong, Jemmi?" Scatha asked one morning when Jemmi rose early and left the bed. Jemmi sighed and shook his head.

"Please," Scatha said, touching his bare arm lightly.

"Do not touch me, woman!" Jemmi snapped.

"Jemmi..." she whispered, hurt.

"Lioness, you are not little any more," Jemmi said, his back to her. He turned around. "I do not want to hurt you, but...." He left the sentence unfinished, shrugging his shoulders. Scatha took a deep breath and closed her eyes.

"Jemmi," she said gently, opening her eyes again. "I am not little any more."

Jemmi took a cautious step forward. Scatha reached out her hands to him, and he took them.

"Jemmi..."

"Do not speak," Jemmi said quietly. "You are my woman."

Scatha nodded and Jemmi kissed her deeply. When all was done, Scatha quietly lay in Jemmi's arms.

"Jemmi?"

"Yes?"

"How do people get married in your home?"

"Just like we did," Jemmi said with a smile. He was falling quickly into sleep.

"Jemmi?"

"Yes?"

"I want our children to be free."

It was the last thing Scatha murmured before falling to sleep. Jemmi sighed sadly, "Me too, Lioness," before he, too, fell to sleep.

In his dreams, Jemmi saw an island wrapped in fog, and on that island, his children played. When he told his dream to Scatha, Scatha smiled and she told him of an island north of her home that was hidden in mist. It was so rarely seen that people said it was impossible to get to. They called it 'The Land of Shadow.'

"When we leave here, we should go there," Jemmi said.

"And how are we to leave?"

"I have an idea."

"And if we do escape, what about your home?"

Jemmi shrugged. "I do not have a home any more. The Crimson Guard burnt it to the ground."

"The island is much colder than here, much colder than you are used to."

"Then it's a good thing I have a wife to keep me warm."

Scatha laughed. "Alright, let's hear this plan of yours."

With Jemmi at the helm, a revolt was planned. Many of the ebony-skinned fighters were hungry for home, and wives of their own. Of the few ghost-skinned, all of them were as proud as the men of the Isle, and eager to prove it. Where the men went after they won over the guards was up to them.

The signal was to come during Scatha's fight. The master had never forgiven Scatha the injury she dealt him, and though she fought well and won often, she was never rewarded as the other fighters were. It seemed fair that the signal should come from her.

After Scatha's victory the following day, amidst the roar of adoring spectators, she hoisted up a spear. She threw it hard into the owner's room – a little walled-off box that overlooked the cage where Scatha fought. The crowd fell into shocked silence. They stared down at the fighter in the cage.

With a great roar, the fighters in the den behind the cage rushed forward. Years of arrogant neglect had rusted the hinges and locks, and hundreds of angry hands pulling at them made them cave easily. They broke through the gate, tore down the cage and surged out of the arena.

The same arrogance that had led to the gates being so easily flung aside also led to the complete incompetence of the soldiers. Some had rushed forward to meet the slaves. Most simply dropped their weapons and ran when faced with the shouting, angry mob of well-muscled, well-seasoned fighters. Before an hour was out, only the master was left. He stood defiantly, waving his crop around and demanding that his slaves return to the dens at once.

"You!" Jemmi shouted at him. "You hurt my woman!"

The master would have laughed, had Jemmi not thrown a knife right into his skull. With a triumphant roar, the crowd left the estate. Freedom awaited them in the desert beyond the estate walls and there, they dispersed. Jemmi and Scatha hugged each other close.

"Now what?" Scatha asked.

Jemmi grinned. "We go home."

Scatha nodded.

"Where is home?" Jemmi asked.

"West," Scatha said. "We go west."

For a year and half Jemmi and Scatha walked. When at last Scatha spied the seas of the channel, she smiled.

"There, Jemmi," she said. "Beyond that sea is the Isle."

"We will need a boat."

That night, Scatha and Jemmi went into the port city. They stole upon a trading ship, hiding themselves well in the loft of the hold. It was risky, but well worth the trouble. They crossed the next morning and, the following night were able to slip away unnoticed.

Scatha's instincts guided her to her father's land. There was nothing left of it. Of the large wooden keep, there remained but one blackened stump. All else had been covered by grass or encroaching forest.

"This is not home any more," Scatha said quietly.

"Come," Jemmi said, taking his wife's hand. "Let us make a new one."

Scatha nodded. They walked to the westernmost sea, a journey of many weeks, and Scatha pointed. "You see that fog?"

"Yes."

"In there is the Land of Shadow. No one lives on that island. We would be safe from the Crimson Guard there."

"Then we must go over."

"How? We have no boat, and we cannot steal one. There are no townships on this coast. They fear it haunted."

"When we must cross a pond," Jemmi said, "we make a raft."

Scatha laughed. "This is no pond!"

"But it is water. Come, woman, help me."

Together Scatha and her husband built a raft of young trees and, using a stone axe, Jemmi carved two paddles. They pushed the raft into the waves and climbed aboard.

"Jemmi," Scatha said as they disappeared in the fog.

"Yes?"

"I want you to know there is no one else I'd rather drown with."

"We will not drown, woman. Now paddle."

Scatha and her husband vanished silently into the mist.

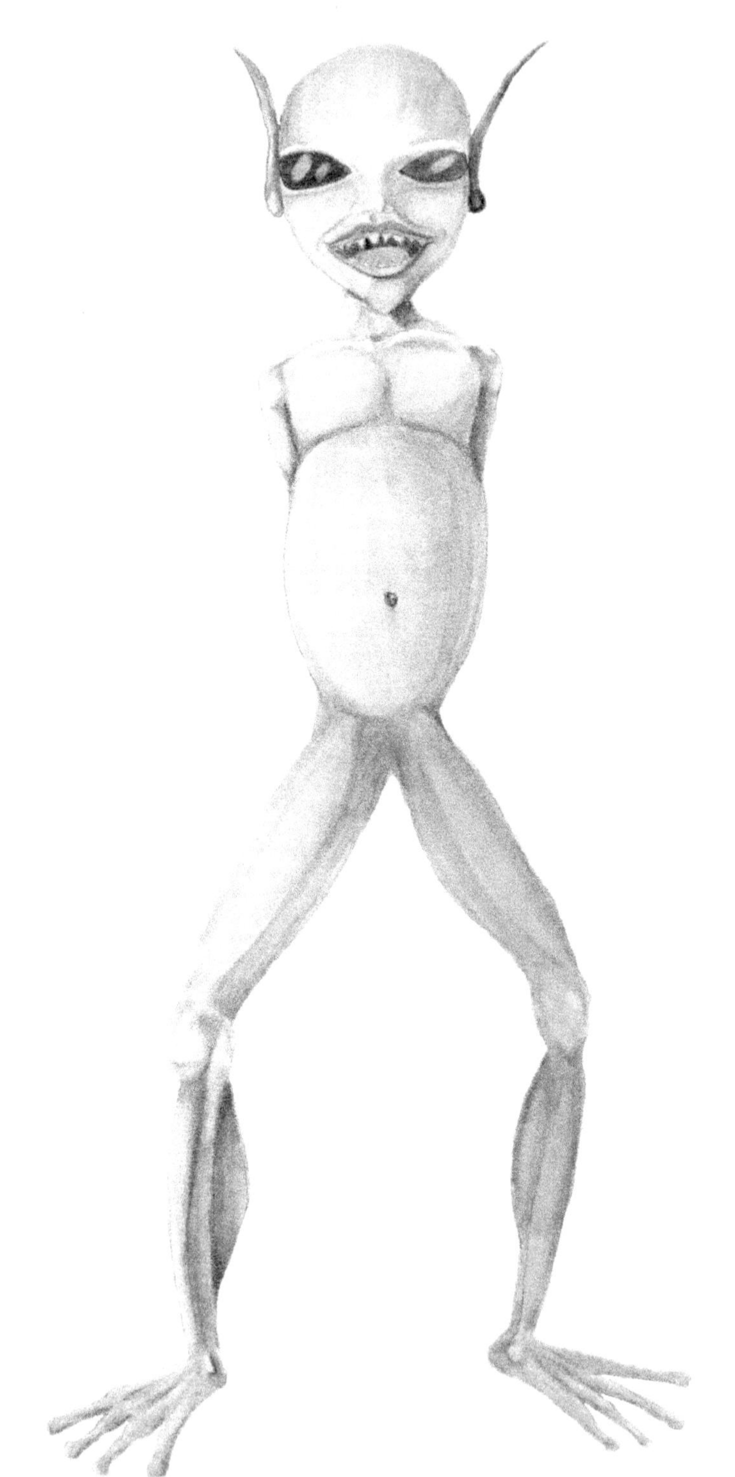

For My Sister

I know you're getting mad
Because my tales are always sad,
So I've written one just for you.
Thus, without more ado:
Once there was a peasant girl,
Very pretty, with a strawberry curl.
She was such a pretty little thing,
And boy, could she ever sing!
She never dreamt she might ever be
Married very happily,
To anyone but the butcher's son,
And goodness knows, he was no fun!
It just so happened one day,
A prince called Randolf passed her way.
He was handsome and brave and strong,
And was in a mind to woo her with song.
His parents were furious, and they fought,
But in the end her hand was sought.
She married her prince joyfully,
And spent 'happily ever after' as royalty.
And so ends my little tale,
With everyone happy, whole, and hale.
I hope it moved you merrily,
But much more importantly,
That you neither sobbed nor sighed,
Because, dear sis, as promised, no one died.

Imp

"Hello?" Hello? Is anyone there? Hello?"

It was such a tiny little voice, so sad and forlorn that I couldn't help but sit up in bed and look around. I shared this room with eight other girls, all of them younger than I. Privacy in an orphanage is a luxury we simply could not afford. In fact, we could not afford anything. The only thing that was my own I had because it was given to me.

It was my grandmother's necklace. Nothing more than a gold charm with a cloudy amethyst in it. It stayed around my neck at all times. The thin gold chain on which it hung broke a long time ago, so now it hung on a black piece of cord. I still had it because I was able to hide it beneath the black dress that all orphans must wear. Otherwise the abbess would have taken it from me. "Pieces of vanity," she called them. "An affront to God," she would tell us.

"Hello? Mistress? Please tell me someone is there?"

"Hello?" I whispered back.

There was a little squeak and then silence.

"Hello?" I whispered a little louder.

Silence.

With an annoyed sigh, I fell back down onto the bed and closed my eyes. I'd be fifteen in a year. When you're fifteen years old, you're no longer welcome at the orphanage. No one wants a child that's almost fully grown. The nuns wouldn't be able to find you parents, and you'd just become more of a burden that you already are.

I was nervous. There were few jobs out there for a girl orphan. Certainly I've been schooled, so I could become a live-in nurse or some such. I didn't particularly want to be a nurse. I wouldn't be allowed to teach. You need to be educated in a special, very expensive school before you're allowed to teach. Not that I would want to teach, but it's a job, and it pays better than nursing.

There were other jobs, of course, if they weren't already filled. Jobs were very scarce these days, and many an orphan ended up on the street, begging for a living. I did not want to be a beggar. I'd rather be a nurse than a beggar, and that's saying something!

"Are you still there?" the tiny voice whispered. I frowned and sat up again. I looked around. All the other children were fast asleep. So was the nun who was supposed to be watching us.

"Yes," I replied.

The voice squeaked in what must have been excitement. "Are you in the purple too?"

In the purple? Whatever could that mean? "I... I don't think so."

"Oh." The voice sounded disappointed. "Where are you then?"

"Where am I? Where are you?"

"I'm in the purple. Where are you?"

"What do you mean 'in the purple'? What is that?"

"Purple is a colour."

"Thank you, I know."

"Then why did you ask? Where are you?"

"I'm in the orphanage."

"What's the orphanage?"

"*An* orphanage is a place for children to go when they have no parents."

"Where are your parents?"

Tears stung my eyes suddenly as I recalled the carriage accident that took place when I was just five. Mother screamed when the road gave way and the carriage toppled over the side of the mountain. I had been riding with the guard on his horse at the time. "They're dead."

"Oh."

There was nothing for a long time, then, "Will you be my friend?"

"How can you ask that? I don't know who you are. I can't even see you."

"I'm in the purple," the voice replied with an impatient sigh.

I rolled my eyes and lay back down. "Well, I'm in a room with eight other girls, and if I am caught awake, I'll be thrashed. So I'm going back to sleep."

"But..."

"No buts. Goodnight."

The voice paused briefly, then said, "No one's wished me a good night for a very long time."

I closed my eyes tight, and before I knew it, I was fast asleep.

I thought it a dream when I awoke in the morning. It had to be either a dream, or I was going mad, for whom else but a madman would hear little voices no one else does? It was a normal day. I went to prayers in the morning. Then I did my chores. It was school for the rest of the day.

It wasn't until the evening 'quiet time,' when we were all studying that the voice spoke again.

"Hello? Are you there?"

"Shh!" I hissed.

There was a tiny little sigh. The silence lasted the better part of half an hour before I heard the voice again.

"I'm bored."

"Be quiet!" I whispered harshly. The nun's head snapped up, and she glared at me. I quickly bent my head down and began to write furiously.

"Do you think...?"

"Be quiet or you will get me into trouble!"

"Miss Erie," the nun said from right beside my desk. I looked up.

"Yes, Sister?"

"Hold out your hand."

I eyed the wooden ruler the nun had in her hand and swallowed hard. "I'm sorry, Sister. I promise I'll be quiet."

"Hold. Out. Your. Hand."

Glumly, I did. The nun took it in hers and held the ruler high. I squeezed my eyes shut and turned away.

Thwack! Thwack! Thwack! The ruler cut across my knuckles as hard as stone. I tried not to make any noise, but I couldn't help sobbing after the first cut.

"Now, perhaps, you will know the meaning of silence."

"Yes, Sister."

"Now go to bed. There will be no supper for you."

My hand aching and stinging both, I packed away my books, tucking them tidily into the desk, and walked from the study room. I paid no heed to the eyes of the other orphans as they followed me out.

"Get back to work!" I heard the nun snap as I raced up the stairs. Once in my room and quite alone, I burst into tears on the bed and cried as hard as I dared without the nuns hearing. When I calmed down a little, that tiny voice spoke to me again.

"I'm sorry."

"I told you to be quiet!" I snapped. "Now my hand is all cut."

"Will you let me out? Perhaps I can help."

"Let you out of where?"

"Out of the purple."

"I don't know where that is."

"It's right here!" the little voice said. There were two little slapping sounds, as if bare feet were jumping on a tiled floor. I felt a tug around my neck with each slap. In surprise, I pulled out the pendant and examined it in the fading sunlight. I gasped when the amethyst blinked at me. It *blinked* at me. Then the eye that was the amethyst pulled back, and inside the purple stone I saw a head peering back at me with large, black eyes.

"How do I let you out?" I whispered.

"Just say 'I release you' and I'll be able to leave."

"Can I not say 'I free you?'"

The creature in the stone squealed. "No! No! Don't say that. That will send me away, and we won't be able to be friends any more!"

"Some friend," I muttered darkly. Holding the pendant up by the black chord I said, "I release you."

There was a small puff of purplish grey smoke and the little creature sprang from the stone with a joyful "Yipee!" It landed on my bed and turned around. I blinked. It was a strange looking little thing, standing no taller than a toddler on skinny, bandy legs that turned outwards like a person who has ridden a horse for too long. Its feet were very, very long, and very, very wide and entirely too large for the body they supported.

The arms were the same way, overly long and skinny, with enormous hands at the end of them. The body was little and round, with a potbelly. On a short skinny neck sat a large round head. It was entirely bald, without eyebrows, even. On either side of its head sat two large, sharply pointed ears. Its eyes were also very large, and bulged a little. The nose was tiny and snobbish, and the mouth was very wide indeed. When the lips parted in a grin, I noted with a start that it had two rows of sharp teeth.

The creature's skin was nut brown from head to toe and though it wore no clothing, it was impossible to tell whether it was a boy creature or a girl creature.

The thing smiled broadly and clapped its enormous hands together.

"I'm out! I'm out! I'm out!" it sang as it clapped and danced around on my blankets, picking its feet up and wiggling its bum strangely.

"Shh!" I hissed. "The nuns will hear you!"

The creature stopped dancing and turned back to me. It looked serious now.

"Let me see your hand," the creature said. I held it out and the creature took it. The hands were calloused, but surprisingly gentle. The already large eyes widened when the creature spied the cuts.

"Oh my. Oh my, my. Oh my, my, my!" it said, stroking gently around the wounds. Surprisingly, it helped with the pain a little. The creature looked up at me. "Would you like me to heal it?"

"There are bandages, but the nuns keep them locked up."

The creature smiled. "I do not need bandages. Here." The creature covered my hand with both of its hands. I felt a strange prickling sensation, then the pain began to ebb away. It only took a moment, but when the creature pulled its hands away, the cuts were gone. All that remained were the bruises.

"I can get rid of those too, if you want."

I shook my head. "The nuns will think it strange that I got hit and have no marks to show for it."

"What did she hit you with?" the creature asked.

"A ruler. Her stupid ruler. I wish it would break and she could never use it again!"

"There, there," the creature said, stroking my hair. "It's alright."

"What is your name?" I asked it.

"I don't have a name, silly," the creature said. "Mistress called me 'Imp.'"

"Mistress?"

"Yes. The woman who put me in the purple. Angry people were banging on her door. She told me to stay quiet. When I asked her for how long, she said 'as long as you possibly can.' So I did. At last I couldn't take it any more, and I had to say something."

"It must have been a very long time, indeed."

"It was. A long, long, long time. I think Mistress has gone now. She was my friend."

"I will be your friend, Imp," I said. "Just as long as you promise to stay quiet when the nuns are around."

Imp looked as if it might cry. "You'll be my friend?"

I nodded. Imp clapped its oversized hands together, then threw its arms around my neck.

"Oh, thank you!" it said. "Thank you, thank you, thank you!"

There was heavy stomping as the children came up the stairs from dinner. I gasped, realising that I had nowhere for Imp to hide. Imp just grinned and dove right back into the amethyst. I hurriedly put on the necklace and tucked it under my gown and collapsed into bed as if I had fallen asleep crying.

The nuns paid me no heed as they ordered the children into bed. They blew out the candles and went back downstairs. When I was sure everyone was settled and asleep, I drew out the necklace and closed it in my fist.

"Goodnight, Imp," I whispered.

"Goodnight, Mistress," the small voice answered back. I smiled contentedly. For the first time in my life, I had a friend.

Imp became my confidant. Whenever I was sad or angry, I'd tell it and it would, in turn, comfort me. I would keep scraps from dinner in my skirt and feed Imp whenever I could. Imp was good company, for a while. Then, one morning, I was woken early by an angry nun. She held in her hands the tiny splintered fragments of her ruler. I stared at them in sleepy surprise.

"This," the nun hissed angrily, "was given to me by the Abbot of Berkshire. It was made from an olive tree branch from the Holy Land. Have you any idea how valuable it was?"

I blinked and shook my head.

"You vile little wretch!" the nun screamed, waking the other girls. They all sat up to watch the scene. "How dare you break my ruler!"

My jaw fell open. "But… but I didn't!"

"Don't lie to me!" the nun screeched.

"But, Sister, I didn't touch your ruler!"

The nun screamed in rage and struck me across the cheek. Tears stung my eyes. She grabbed me by the elbow and dragged me down to where the abbess slept. Without bothering to knock, she barged in on the abbess, who was kneeling by her bed in prayer.

"Abbess," the nun said sharply at the surprised woman. "This horrid little snipe has broken the ruler your brother gave me."

"No… I…"

"Silence!" the nun screamed, shaking me hard.

"Show me," the abbess said, hauling her considerable weight off the floor. The nun threw the splintered pieces of the ruler onto the abbess' bed. Slowly, like watching a tomato ripen, the abbess' face turned red. She looked at me, her pudgy features twisted in anger.

"You vile sinner!" she shrieked.

"But I…"

"Silence!" the abbess roared, stomping her foot. "Your soul is too corrupt for even the sisters to save you. We cannot house you." The abbess turned to the nun. "Throw her out into the street."

I was dumbfounded. I was not fifteen yet. I could not be thrown out onto the street! The nun nodded sharply. She dragged me from the abbess' room and, ignoring my protests and declarations of innocence, threw me bodily out the door of the orphanage. I landed with a painful crack on my hands and knees. I stood in my nightdress and turned. Helpless, I watched as the nun slammed the door shut and heard the depressing click of the lock.

Not knowing what else to do, and my heart pounding in anxious fear, I ran. I didn't know to where I was running. I kept bumping into people, and they would all look down at me with angry faces and yell at me. I ran and ran and ran until I found a quiet place – a small alley just off the end of the market. I slid to the ground, buried my head in my knees and cried.

It was not long before I felt strong fingers stroking my head.

"Mistress," Imp said sadly. "Oh, Mistress. Don't worry."

"Oh!" I sobbed. "What am I supposed to do now?"

"Would you like me to go back and break something else?"

I looked up at Imp's dark eyes. "What do you mean, 'break something else'?"

"Well, she hit you, and you said you wanted her ruler broken, so...."

"That was you? You broke it?"

Imp nodded.

"Why would you do such a thing? This is all your fault!"

"But... you..."

"I hate you!" I railed. Imp flinched as if it had been hit. "I'm setting you free."

"No!" Imp cried. "No! Don't!"

"I..."

"No!"

"Free..."

"Mistress, please!"

"You."

Imp was pulled backwards and disappeared into nothingness with an anguished wail. I burst into tears again. I was scared, angry and, now, friendless. I curled up on the dirty ground. I slept there that night, and the next, and the one after that, until hunger roused me into action. I stood shakily and wandered out into the market.

I spent the next few months begging on the streets. I was so hungry in the first week that I had to sell my pendant to get enough to eat. The owner of the store did not seem to care that I cried as I handed the pendant over. The money I received for it didn't last the week.

I stole food when I didn't make enough money to pay for it. I wasn't a very successful thief, and often went hungry. I would return to my little alleyway to sleep and to cry. Once, after a week and a half without food, I woke to find a small loaf of bread beside my arm. It had a large bite taken out of it, but was otherwise fresh. I picked it up and tears stung my eyes.

"Imp?" I called, but there was no answer. "Oh, Imp. I miss you so. I'm so sorry." And I wept again.

After three months on the street, I gave up. I sat in my alleyway and did not move for days. One day, though, there was a loud fanfare of trumpets and a great cheer. Though I was so hungry I might faint, curiosity got the better of me and I squeezed my way through the crowd to see what the fuss was about.

There was a parade. The royal family had come to town on a visit. The king and queen were kindly rulers, and because they were generous but firm, the land prospered and they were well loved. However, they were childless. The queen had not been able to conceive. Yet the king loved her so much that he ignored his advisors and refused to put her aside in favour of a more fertile mistress.

They rode now in an open carriage and smiled at the crowd as they waved. The crowd waved and cheered in return. The carriage had almost reached where I was standing when someone shoved me hard. I fell forward, tumbling down in a flail of limbs, and I rolled.

"Stop!" I heard someone shriek. The carriage carrying the royal couple halted, the iron-trimmed wheel stopping just millimetres from my head. I turned my spinning head to look back at the crowd, and spied a small, nut brown shape vanish into the walls of the building behind the crowd.

"Imp?" I whispered before the world went black.

I woke up in a large, soft bed, with purple silk sheets. The smell of spiced soup wafted in and my stomach growled. It felt like my stomach would eat itself. I doubled over in pain and groaned.

"Heavens!" a gentle female voice said. "You're awake."

I felt a cool, soft hand touch my forehead.

"You must be hungry," the voice said.

"I want Imp," I murmured.

"Hush now," the voice said. "We have some broth and fruit. Sit up now."

I tried. I honestly did. Nothing happened. The woman who was looking after me wrapped an arm around my shoulders and helped me up. My body was all floppy and wouldn't stay up of its own accord. The woman leant my weight against her and soon I felt something warm touch my lips. I licked them to discover the best soup I have ever tasted. The woman fed me until I could eat no more, then leant me back on the bed to sleep.

"She was awake just now," I heard the woman say. Then a deeper masculine voice spoke.

"The doctor said that she was too far gone at this juncture. It wouldn't matter what we did. Don't get your hopes up, my love."

And that was all I heard.

It must have been later that night when I felt familiar calloused hands take my own.

"Imp," I whispered. "Is that you?"

"Shh, Mistress," a tiny voice said. "You are very weak. You must rest."

"Imp, I'm so sorry. I don't hate you."

"There, there, Mistress. It will be alright."

"It won't." My strength was fading quickly. "The doctor said..." That was all I had the strength to say. I felt two calloused hands touch my stomach, and then all sensation faded away.

I was certain I had died. Then, after a time, I heard voices. A man was speaking. I tried hard to make out what he was saying.

"... and her colour seems a little better. I don't understand it. She should have died days ago."

"Your Majesty," another voice said.

"What is it?"

"Beggin' your pardon, but the Lord Steward says some food's missin'."

I smiled. Imp.

"Hello," the voice that spoke first said gently. "Do you know about the missing food?"

"Imp," I mumbled in reply.

"What did she say?" the familiar female voice said.

The first voice laughed. "She said that an imp took the food."

The woman laughed also. "She is getting better then!"

"Yes she is. If you keep feeding her, she'll be able to walk in a couple of weeks."

"Oh, doctor! Thank you so much!"

"I'll stay until she's walking. You never know with things like this. I'd like to be on call in case she takes a turn for the worst."

"I promise I shall keep you informed of everything."

"Very good, then. I think you should feed her now. I hear her stomach grumbling."

The woman did just that.

A few days passed before I opened my eyes. I could have done so before now, but I was terrified to find that this was all a dream. When I did finally open my eyes, they met with a pair of kind brown eyes in the beautiful, round face of a woman. The woman smiled.

"Hello." Her voice was kind.

Too shy to do much else, I ventured a small smile in return.

"I am Rosalee."

I blinked. "Queen Rosalee?"

The woman smiled. "The same. I have food coming. My, but your stomach is loud!"

"I'm sorry, your Majesty."

"Oh don't be sorry!" Rosalee said with a smile and a dismissive wave. "And please, call me Rosalee. At least while we're in private."

I nodded.

"What is your name?"

"Miss Erie."

"And what is your first name, Miss Erie?"

Tears stung my eyes. No one had cared to know my first name since my parents died. The nuns avoided using first names whenever possible. I had always been known as Miss Erie.

"Catherine," I said.

"That is a beautiful name."

"Thank you," I said, my face flushing. The door opened then, and a very handsome man with dark hair and blue eyes walked in, carrying a tray of soup with freshly buttered bread.

"Hello," he said kindly.

"Hello."

The man put the tray of food down beside my bed and stood behind Rosalee. He placed his hands on her shoulders.

"Tell me, Catherine?" she said, her eyes shining. "Have you ever dreamt of being a princess?"

That night, when all was settled and agreed upon, I lay in bed and stared up at the canopy, wondering at my good fortune. Something rustled at the end of my bed. I sat up. There, bathed in moonlight, stood Imp, hands clasped shyly behind the creature's back.

"Imp!" I exclaimed. "Oh Imp!" I crawled forward and drew the creature into a fierce embrace and started sobbing. "I've missed you so much!"

"Do you like it here?" Imp asked.

"I do! I love it!"

"Then... am I forgiven?"

I started to laugh through my tears. "Oh, Imp! You were forgiven the moment I got mad at you! I'm so sorry I sent you away. Will you stay?"

Imp pulled away and shook its oversized head. "I can't."

"Why not?"

"You set me free."

"Oh."

Imp sighed. "But we'll still be friends, right?"

"Of course!" I replied immediately. "So be sure to visit. Often."

Imp nodded. It looked at me sadly for a moment, before snapping its fingers and vanishing into smoke.

"Good night, Princess," I heard a tiny voice say as the smoke dissipated.

"Good night, Imp. Farewell."

I never did see Imp again, but I knew that the little nut-brown creature was around. Food went missing fairly regularly. It was never very much, perhaps enough to feed a small child.

When I turned twenty, I met Prince George of Rathonwy. He was so handsome that he quite took my breath away. We were married the following summer.

I received a wonderful surprise on my wedding day. I unwrapped a small gift that had been covered in little rags and tied with twine. I gasped as I saw my amethyst pendant glistening therein, sitting beautifully on a thin gold chain. I knew it was from Imp.

I've never taken it off since.

Queen Catherine put down her pen and shook her hand. She had been writing her life's story all night and her hand was quite cramped. The door of her bedroom creaked open, and four-year-old Princess Adelaide wandered in, bleary-eyed and yawning.

"Adelaide, child!" the queen said in surprise as she spied her granddaughter wandering into the room. "Whatever are you doing up?"

"I was chastised for not wishing you goodnight," Adelaide answered, her missing teeth giving the young princess a thick lisp. "'It is the nicest thing in the world to be wished a goodnight,' he said."

"Who said?"

"Why, my bestest friend," the princess replied, as if surprised the queen had to ask. "Imp."

Mr. Campbell

Once upon a time ... "No, no, that's been taken!"

There once lived a beautiful Princess, who was locked in a tower... "No! That one's taken too!"

The man threw down his quill and stood. He paced his tiny studio apartment, muttering dark curses.

"I hate you, Brothers Grimm!" he spat suddenly, stomping his foot hard on the creaky floorboard. The annoyed tenants directly below answered with a thump of their own. The man shrieked and threw up his hands.

"I can't work like this!"

He spun on his heel and grabbed his cloak to ward off the evening chill. He stomped angrily downstairs and out the door.

"Hello, Mad Jack!" a child playing on the street called.

"Mad Jack indeed," the man muttered.

His name was not Jack. It was Gregory Campbell, and he was a writer. Or so he called himself. He'd never actually had anything published, but that was not the point. Editors, he had declared to himself, knew nothing of the art of writing, else they'd have published him long ago. Now almost grey-haired, Mr. Campbell was working on the masterpiece that would make editors everywhere envious.

If only he could figure out what it was.

Mr. Campbell mused on this as he stomped his way across the road and down the lane. The poorly tended cobblestones played havoc on Mr. Campbell's ankles, but he was too proud for a cane. So he muttered and cursed to himself as he hobbled down alleys and streets until he came to the shore.

It was a pebbly shore and thus not very popular. Mr. Campbell felt at peace here. The gentle hissing of the waves and the smell of salt was soothing to him. Even the gulls, which annoyed the everyday beach-goer, found a friend in Mr. Campbell.

He found a suitable rock, sat on it, and watched the sun sink over the waves.

"Some days," he said to no one in particular, "I wish I were a fish, that I could live in the ocean I love so much, and bear witness to all its wonders."

"Very well," a tiny voice answered.

Suddenly the world went quite dark, and Mr. Campbell could not breathe. He squirmed in panic, only to realise that someone had covered him with a cloth. It was very loose, and he found he could squirm out of it easily. It was no easier to breathe free of the cloth. Mr. Campbell noted that he was lying on his side, looking up at the sky.

He tried to put his hands beneath his body to push himself up, only to find that he couldn't reach. Something was terribly wrong. It took a turn for the worst when Mr. Campbell spied a giant seagull hovering over him, eyeing him with hungry curiosity.

"Oh!" he heard someone exclaim. "Shoo! Shoo!"

Enormous arms waved into Mr. Campbell's view, frightening the gull off. Then an enormous face peered down at him.

"Don't worry, little fishy," the girl, who sounded very young, said. "I'll put you back in the water."

"We could eat it," another voice shouted from the distance.

"No!" she shrieked as she picked Mr. Campbell up. The girl ran with him in her arms into the sea and gently lowered him down. With a swift flick of his tail, Mr. Campbell vanished into the waves.

"Good luck, little fishy," the girl said.

Mr. Campbell swam frantically for several moments before it occurred to him that he was several feet under the surface of the water, and he was breathing. He stopped swimming and looked around him. As he turned, he caught sight of something silvery in his peripheral vision. He turned to see what it was. A tail. He spun around in a frantic circle, the tail ever eluding him. Then Mr. Campbell realised.

Heavens above! Mr. Campbell thought. I'm a fish!

Then he screamed.

That was an error. His scream caught the attention of another fish. A larger fish. A hungry fish.

"Hello," the fish said from behind Mr. Campbell. Mr. Campbell spun around.

"H-h-h-hel-l-l-o," Mr. Campbell stuttered back.

"Food!" the bigger fish roared gleefully. It rushed forward. Mr. Campbell squealed and dove down.

"Come back, food!" the fish cried as it dove after him.

"Aaaaaaaaaaaaaaahhhhhhhhhhh!" Mr. Campbell screamed as he

careened around rocks on the sea floor in a desperate bid to escape. He felt himself pulled sideways. Everything went black as he was pulled into a dark crevice. A dark fin wrapped around his mouth to muffle his renewed screams.

"Hush, or he'll find us both!"

"Where are you, food?" the fish that had been chasing Mr. Campbell called out as he swam lazily around the rock-strewn sea floor. "Here fishy, fishy, fishy!"

Mr. Campbell's racing heart stopped dead at the sight of the bigger fish as it sailed smoothly past the crevice where he was hiding. The large fish seemed not to see him and swam lazily on. At length, the fish's voice faded away. The strange fish that had saved Mr. Campbell kept him in that crevice for a while longer before cautiously swimming out for a look.

Mr. Campbell noted that the fish was black and sleek, with many fins that were long and floated in the water like silk in a breeze. Once out into the light, the black fish sparkled with flecks of gold. It turned around and regarded the crevice with amber eyes. As far as fish went, this one was very pretty.

"You can come out now," it said with a voice that was light and smooth and feminine.

Mr. Campbell slowly exited the crevice, taking careful stock of his surroundings. What once appeared to be a barren sea floor was now teeming with life. Fish of all shapes and sizes swam about, going about their fishy business. Finally, Mr. Campbell turned to the black fish.

"Thank you," he said earnestly, "for saving me."

"You aren't from around here, are you?" the black fish asked.

"No. Um... I'm Mr. Campbell," Mr. Campbell said, extending his fin as if he was to shake hands. The black fish stared at it before answering. She did not take it.

"My name is Aronwyl. Princess Aronwyl."

"Princess?"

"Yes, that's right. That's the third time Starrick's henchmen have trespassed in the last week! We must go tell my father." Without waiting for Mr. Campbell, Aronwyl turned with a flick of her tail and was gone.

"Whoa, wait!" Mr. Campbell called, giving chase. Aronwyl was very fast and Mr. Campbell found himself out of breath when he finally caught up to her. She had stopped just before a long stretch of white sand. Mr. Campbell stopped too. His breath caught.

Before him stretched a long lawn of sand, in the middle of which stood an enormous castle of rock. Its many-spired columns reached high up into the blue water and, at this time of night, it was framed by moonlight. Behind the castle waved a forest of seaweeds.

"Come on," Aronwyl said, darting forward again. They paused again at the entrance to the enormous portcullis, where two soldier crabs stood guard.

"'Oo goes there," said one.

"Don't be daft, Brackfi," Aronwyl said. "It's me."

"Oh, er, sorry, your Highness. Didn't recognise you, what with this dark and all." He turned and called back through the bars of the portcullis. "Oi! Open up in there. The princess is home!"

The portcullis opened slowly and Aronwyl swam through, Mr. Campbell in tow. If Mr. Campbell had been astounded before, he was utterly gob-smacked now. The portcullis opened to reveal an expansive courtyard where crabs marched sideways in small groups. A massive stable filled with seahorses that neighed and nickered in restless sleep stood off to one side.

Small shrimp were carefully tending the sand and the walls of the court-yard, as well as the well-trimmed weeds that lined those walls. Aronwyl seemed oblivious to the splendour around her. Mr. Campbell was not.

He lagged behind the princess, trying to take in all he saw. She disappeared into the castle and Mr. Campbell rushed to find her once again.

"Keep up," Aronwyl said sharply.

"Yes. Sorry," said Mr. Campbell.

Together they wound their way through halls of mother of pearl, lit with the eerie glow of bioluminescent torches and the occasional window allowing the diffused light of the moon into the castle. Mr. Campbell was thoroughly lost by the time they entered the throne room.

Of all the magnificent buildings that man had ever made, none matched the splendour of the throne room. Three chandeliers of bioluminescent light shone brightly in the ceiling of mother of pearl. The floor was dark stone that shone like glass, and the walls were lined with pearls.

Two open oysters sat on a raised dais. In one rested a delicate gold fish, with flowing fins just like Aronwyl's. In the other sat a massive black fish, with a fierce face and silvery eyes. In one fin he held a trident and on his head rested a crown of bright red coral and pearl.

"Aronwyl!" the gold fish said. "Thank goodness you're home safe!"

"Who is this?" the black fish demanded, pointing his trident at Mr. Campbell.

"Mother, father," Aronwyl greeted. "This is Mr. Campbell."

Mr. Campbell tried to bow, but was not very successful. "Good evening, Your Majesties."

"Why is he here?"

"Your daughter saved my life, your Majesties," Mr. Campbell replied. "I had nowhere else to go, so I followed her."

"Your pet cannot stay," the king said.

"We will deal with him later. I have important news. Starrick's henchmen have trespassed in the east for the third time this week."

"We know," the king replied. "There have also been four attacks in the south; an entire colony destroyed and three others very near to it. The refugees are hiding in the forest right now, and all signs say that Starrick is headed this way. We are mobilising. We will be ready for battle by dawn."

"You think they mean to storm the castle?"

"They do, and soon. They are moving quickly, and have the current on their side."

Aronwyl sighed. "I'll suit up in a moment."

"No, my daughter. It is not right that you fight. You will go to the forest and stay there with the refugees until the battle is over."

"I will not!" Aronwyl snapped. "This is my kingdom too, father. I have as much a right to defend it as you!"

"This will be your kingdom when I am gone. If anything should happen to you the kingdom would be lost altogether. You will do as I say."

"But...."

"Enough! Captain!" the king roared. In a few moments, a large crab scuttled into the throne room.

"Your Majesty?"

"You will escort Princess Aronwyl and her pet to the refugee camp and keep her there. War is upon us, and I would not see my daughter harmed."

"Yes, your Majesty. Come, your Highness."

With a resigned sigh, Aronwyl turned and swam slowly from the room, the crab scuttling along behind, offering kind words that did nothing for the princess' disposition. Mr. Campbell turned to follow, but the king cleared his throat pointedly. Mr. Campbell turned back.

"Mr. Campbell," the king said. "I have a favour to ask of you."

"I shall do what I can, your Majesty."

"If I know the captain but a little, at the first blow of the war shell, his sense of duty will compel him to battle. I need you to ensure that Aronwyl stays put."

"I will try, your Majesty."

"There is no try."

"Yes, your Majesty." Mr. Campbell turned and left the throne room. "But I'm only a writer," he whispered.

It was a good two hours travel to the forest and the refugee camp hidden inside. The number of fish there saddened Mr. Campbell, most of them mothers with children still latched at their sides. Several other fish were gravely injured.

"The true cost of war," the captain said when he scuttled to a stop.

"Captain," Aronwyl said, spinning to face him. "I command you to take me back at once!"

"If it didn't work in the time it took to get here, it's not going to work now, your Highness. I have my orders."

"My father is out there fighting! I have to help him!"

"Be that as it may..."

The war shell blew a long mournful note. The fighting had begun.

The captain stayed as long as he could, but it was not even half an hour before he started fretting.

"Don't move," he commanded the princess. "I'll be right back." With that, the captain scuttled off, moving quickly for a creature that ran sideways.

"The hell I will!" Aronwyl grated. In an instant, she was off into the night.

"Hey!" Mr. Campbell called after her. "Wait! Waaaaaaaaaiiit!"

It was no use. Desperate, Mr. Campbell took off after her. He was nowhere near as fast and though he made good time, he arrived much too late.

The fighting had ground to a halt. On one side of the sand lawn was the king and his fine troops. On the other, Starrick and his motley horde of savages. Starrick himself looked like a paler, smaller version of the king. In one fin he held Aronwyl and in the other, a crude, but very sharp, trident pressed against the princess' gills.

"What's it to be?" Starrick demanded. "Your kingdom, or your daughter."

"Oh no," whispered Mr. Campbell.

"Uncle, please!" Aronwyl begged, struggling a little. Starrick pressed the trident harder.

"Stop moving, sweetling," he crooned.

The sight of poor Aronwyl threatened so caused Mr. Campbell's temper to overflow. With a roar, he charged forward and crashed bodily into Starrick. The startled Starrick simultaneously dropped his trident and released Aronwyl, who promptly swam and hid behind her father.

"Get him!" Starrick roared as Mr. Campbell darted away. In an instant the entire army was chasing Mr. Campbell, who was swimming desperately for his life.

"Attack!" roared the king and soon Mr. Campbell was forgotten as the battle was re-engaged.

Mr. Campbell saw none of it. He was far too busy swimming away from a familiar thug.

"Food!" bellowed the fish as it chased Mr. Campbell around the sand lawn.

"Oh no he isn't!" Seemingly appearing from nowhere, Aronwyl impaled the fish with her father's trident.

"Thank you," puffed Mr. Campbell.

"I'm returning the favour."

"Victory!" the king roared and Aronwyl and Mr. Campbell turned to see the remnants of Starrick's army fleeing.

"Oh, thank heavens!" Mr. Campbell sighed.

The kingdom celebrated for a week. As Aronwyl's saviour, Mr. Campbell was the centre of a great deal of attention. An unpublished writer on dry land, he had no idea how to handle the fame, and escaped one evening into the stunning castle gardens.

"Mr. Campbell?" Aronwyl queried from behind him.

"Your Highness!"

"Please, call me Aronwyl."

"Aronwyl." It pleased Mr. Campbell to call her by name.

"You know," Aronwyl said, swimming slowly at Mr. Campbell's side as they wandered through the gardens. "With all these celebrations, I never got the chance to thank you properly."

"Oh, you don't...." Mr. Campbell's sentence was cut short by a lightly placed fin on his lips.

"Thank you," Aronwyl said, before kissing him gently. Mr. Campbell was surprised, and greatly pleased until he remembered his old life. Mr. Campbell froze.

"What's wrong?"

"Aronwyl, there's something about me you should know."

"Oh?"

"I am not a fish."

"You're not a fish." It was clear from her tone that Aronwyl did not believe him.

"No. I mean, I am at the moment, but I wasn't always... I was a writer, you see."

"A what?"

"I writer. I wrote things."

"What?"

"Here, let me show you." Mr. Campbell scrawled marks in the sand with his fin. "This is the word 'sand' in writing."

Aronwyl simply stared at the word.

"I was a man. I lived in a town near the sea... never *in* the sea."

Aronwyl gasped. "You are a human?"

"Yes."

"Oh no!"

Mr. Campbell had never known that fish could weep. "Aronwyl, please listen. There's something I must do on land. Something I started and must finish."

"You want to leave?"

"Yes, but only for a short while."

"Oh."

"Please, Aronwyl, I want to come back. I do. When I'm done. Will you wait for me?"

Aronwyl was silent for a while. "You will return?"

"Yes. I promise."

At length Aronwyl nodded. "Then I will wait."

Mr. Campbell was certain he had heard no sweeter words in his life. He kissed Aronwyl.

That night, Aronwyl explained to her father that she was in love, and that Mr. Campbell was, in fact, a man and must return to the land of men for one final task before returning forevermore to the ocean.

The king took some convincing, but it was not long before he called for Moray. Moray, Mr. Campbell soon learnt, was a particularly wise eel. He slithered into court and Mr. Campbell noted that many fish flinched away from him.

Moray stopped dead at the sight of Mr. Campbell.

"You," Moray said in a deep voice, "are not a fish."

"I did not believe it until now," the king said with a shake of his head.

"No," Mr. Campbell replied honestly. "I am not."

"What do you want?" Moray asked him.

"There is something I need to do on land, as a man. Just one thing. But I want to return... And be with Aronwyl."

"A man in love with a fish," Moray said with a laugh. "How remarkable."

"A fish in love with a fish," Mr. Campbell retorted.

"Indeed."

"Can you do it?"

"For a price."

"What price?" the king asked.

Moray smiled. "A new home. Mine is much too small. This palace should do, I think."

Aronwyl gasped.

"No," said Mr. Campbell. "I'll not bargain away their home for a small matter of unfinished business. The price is too high. I'll stay and leave it be."

"Very well then," Moray said. He turned to leave. He reached the door of the throne room before stopping. After a moment, he turned. "I'll do it for free."

"You will?" Aronwyl breathed.

"Love is a rare gift," Moray replied. "To have seen it first-hand is payment enough." Moray then produced two pearls, one black and one white. "You must swim to the surface, fish-man. Then swallow the black pearl. You will have three days, and three days only. If you fail to return to the water by the third sunrise, you will never be able to return."

"I understand."

"Good. Then when you are ready, walk into the sea as far as you dare and swallow the white pearl. You will return to your beloved precisely as you are now."

"I'll do it."

"Very good." Moray handed Mr. Campbell the pearls. "Hurry now."

With an escort that included the king himself, Mr. Campbell and Aronwyl swam up to the surface of the water.

"I will wait for you," Aronwyl promised. Mr. Campbell nodded and swallowed the black pearl. The effect was so sudden that Mr. Campbell almost dropped the white pearl. He managed to catch it at the last moment, before the waves stole it away. He had caught it with a hand; a human hand. His head broke the surface and Mr. Campbell swam as fast as he could to shore.

It was first light. No one would be awake yet. So, though he was completely naked, Mr. Campbell did not fear being spied as he strode out of the water. His clothes remained on the rock. Perhaps passers-by felt that they belonged to a man who had gone bathing, and so were best left where they were.

Mr. Campbell dressed hurriedly, not bothering with his shoes, and then ran home. The cobblestones were cold and painful, but Mr. Campbell ignored them. He rushed up the stairs to his apartment and ran inside, slamming the door shut.

The sun broke over the horizon.

"Sunrise one," Mr. Campbell muttered to himself. He sat down, grabbed his quill and a piece of paper and began to write.

Of all the places on this earth, of all the worlds that man could dream of, there exists nothing more splendiferous than the depths of the ocean. And no animal is more remarkable than the seemingly humble fish...

Mr. Campbell wrote, and wrote, and wrote. He neither ate nor slept, nor did he answer his door when the landlady came knocking. He sat in his chair, frantically recalling his adventures beneath the waves. For two whole days, Mr. Campbell sat and wrote.

It was almost first light when he blew on the last page to dry the ink. He flipped the pages over and on the back of the title page, he wrote:

To Aronwyl, my beloved.

Then he wrote his landlady a letter, saying he was leaving and never returning, and whatever possessions remained in his apartment were now hers, but for the manuscript on his desk. He asked that she might deliver it to a publisher on his behalf, and should it sell, any profits made be given to a charity of her choosing.

Then, with no time to spare, Mr. Campbell raced out of his apartment and back down the cobbled streets to the ocean. Not caring for the clothes he wore, he waded out into the waves up to his shoulders and, drawing the white pearl from his pocket, he swallowed it, vanishing beneath the waves where, as promised, Aronwyl waited for him.

As it happened, Mr. Campbell's story was wildly popular and, as a woman of honour, the landlady offered the profits to aid fishers' widows. Of Mr. Campbell there was never another sign. It was quite the mystery, for all they found of Mr. Campbell was his cloak, washed ashore in the morning light.

Strange Lands

Have you never desired
To hoist sail and travel?
To seek strange lands,
Speak strange tongues,
And know wonderment besides?
Have you never dreamt
Of adventure and mystery?
Of finding new worlds,
Of unfamiliar territory,
Lost, but wholly enthralled?
I have heard of countless lands
Of weeping women
And laughing men.
Where black sheep live,
That when spun around, turn white.
I have heard of stunning isles
Paved in shining gold,
Where the women teach
Men the arts of war.
And all stay young evermore.
I wish to see strange lands,
To roam them and witness
All I possibly can.
For now I must be content
With the journeys of my dreams.

The Taming of Man I

Cysgod Mawr limped through the smouldering terrain. In the blink of an eye, her entire pack had been destroyed. That she alone escaped was a cruel twist of fate. She was young, an alpha female newly made. Now, she was wounded and friendless.

The enormous black hound turned her sleek muzzle skyward and howled. Were there any other hounds around, even her smaller kin, wolves, they would answer. No dog of any kind could resist the call of a black hound.

Silence.

Cysgod Mawr growled and limped a few steps before stopping. A high-pitched wail pierced the grey-brown skies. The black hound shook her coat, ash falling everywhere. It was an exercise in futility. Ash was still raining from the sky.

The wail sounded again. Cysgod Mawr could not contain her curiosity and she trotted in uneven steps towards the sound. The smell of blood assaulted her nostrils. It was thick and rank, detectable even through the dense cloud of ash rain.

Cysgod Mawr skirted past a lava flow that had not yet cooled properly, feeling the heat singe her sooty black coat. She growled ineffectually at it, cursing its existence in her ancient tongue. No sooner had she rounded the bulbous edge of the flow than her weary red eyes fell upon a scene of intense carnage.

Human bodies lay everywhere in a small crater. Many crushed by falling stones and now coated in a thick layer of ash. Only one of their crudely built shelters remained standing, and it was on fire, slowly devoured by the creeping lava.

By the body of a woman, who had been neatly crushed by a boulder, sat a young boy. He could not be much older than four or five. Cysgod Mawr sat at the edge of the crater and observed the human pup for a moment. He was naked, covered in ash, and suffered a severe burn on his left shin.

In his tiny hands, he held an arm torn from the body of the woman crushed beneath the rock. He held it and wailed, tears streaking through the ash on his cheeks. The lava flow that had set the hutch on fire moved slowly down the side of the crater. The boy moved not at all. The scent of blood and worse now mingled with burning flesh as the lava slowly consumed the bodies closest to it.

The scene brought the sharp memory of her own pups, killed at just three weeks by the same volcano that destroyed the boy's pack. Cysgod Mawr was moved. She slid down the crater's edge, despite the sharp pain in her flank and trotted over to the boy.

"Human pup," she said. The boy must not have heard her, for he continued to wail, his eyes tightly shut.

Cysgod Mawr whined and licked the boy's face. That got his attention. The boy turned and stared at the enormous black hound standing before him. He blinked stupidly, too shocked to be afraid.

"Little pup," the black hound said again, "soon this crater will fill with burning stone. You must leave."

The boy simply stared, his eyes a striking shade of deep blue. Cysgod Mawr could feel the heat from the gelatinous liquid rock as it oozed closer.

"Do you hear me, human pup?"

The boy nodded.

"Then come with me. I will take you away from this place."

There was no alternative for the boy. He looked lovingly down at the arm he held and stroked the skin before putting it down. He struggled to his feet. He barely reached Cysgod Mawr's chest.

"You are very small, little pup."

It was all the black hound said before trotting off. The boy stumbled after her, and together they scrambled up the rocky slope of the crater. Cysgod Mawr yelped in agony as the effort lengthened the sizeable gash in her right flank. The boy looked over, his blue eyes calm, and pressed a comforting hand onto Cysgod Mawr's shoulder.

"I am alright," she said. "We must leave this place. The angry mountain may lose her temper again. Can you walk?"

The boy nodded and the pair stumbled south.

For an entire week they walked through ash rain. It was sometimes so thick that the boy could not see an inch before his face and had to hold onto Cysgod Mawr's tail. They would sleep wherever they could find shelter. They had been fortunate enough to find a relatively dry cave one evening and so could sleep without the oppressive risk of ash coating their lungs.

The enormous black hound found no shortage of food. Injured animals were scattered widely, even days away from the volcano. The boy would not eat, turning his head at the thought of consuming raw flesh. Instead, Cysgod Mawr offered her teats to the boy, whimpering her grief quietly as she thought of her own pups.

The eighth day of walking saw the thinning of the ash rain, and the first set of trees that had not been flattened by falling rocks and debris.

"Shelter," Cysgod Mawr said with satisfaction. "We may find water here too." The black hound eyed the boy with her steady red gaze. "You need a bath."

The boy's mouth quirked as he looked at Cysgod Mawr. She looked nothing more than a walking mound of ash.

That night, they slept beneath the sloping branches of an ash-laden tree. The sprawling branches protected the pair from the falling ash and they rested long that night. The boy snuggled in close and Cysgod Mawr licked his face clean.

"I am glad I am with you, little pup," she said. She settled her great head down.

"My name is Gruffudd," the boy murmured.

"A lordly name," the black hound replied, her words touched by a small smile.

"You are Cysgod Mawr, of the black hounds of Annwfyn."

"I am."

"My clan was afraid of you."

"And so they should have been. Now sleep, Gruffudd. We still have a ways to travel before we are safe from the angry mountain."

Gruffudd, smiling, did just that.

The following morning found the pair gently, waking them from their slumber with the first hint of sunlight they had seen for days. It did not last long, but was long enough to energise them.

"Up, pup," Cysgod Mawr said brusquely. "There is food to be found and we are not safe from the angry mountain yet."

"Why did the mountain become angry?" Gruffudd asked plaintively as they walked.

"I do not know," the black hound replied. She lifted her muzzle and sniffed tentatively at the air.

"The holy man used to say that the earth would get angry at us if we did something wrong; if we hunted too much or were careless in our actions. I don't think we did anything wrong..."

"Hush," Cysgod Mawr growled. "You are scaring away the food! I cannot hunt with all this racket!"

"Sorry," Gruffudd whispered. Cysgod Mawr did not reply. She remained perfectly still, her ears pricked and her keen eyes scanning the trees. Gruffudd quickly became impatient.

"What are we hunting?" he whispered hoarsely.

Whatever it was, it had heard and the soft sounds of a fleeing hoofed animal echoed through the trees. Cysgod Mawr turned her head to Gruffudd and narrowed her red eyes at him. Her lips parted in a silent snarl. Gruffudd drew back.

Without a word, Cysgod Mawr turned and stalked angrily away. Afraid that he was now unwanted, Gruffudd did not follow. He stood in the now silent forest, frozen, until he could no longer hear the black hound's footfalls.

Without the massive hound for company, Gruffudd felt terribly alone. He let his weight fall to the soft earth with a thump, and buried his head in his arms.

"Mamma," he sobbed.

"Well, well, well," said a sly voice. "What have we here?"

Gruffudd looked up in surprise. He had thought he was alone. His blue eyes widened in fear. Tawny wolves, their coats smattered with ash rain, surrounded him.

"A pup without its mummy," a wolf sneered.

Gruffudd stood swiftly. "Stay away!" he warned. "Or I'll... I'll..."

"You'll what?"

The truth is, there was nothing that Gruffudd could do. He was a scrawny boy with nothing in his defence. He had not the sharp claws and teeth the wolves had. He did not even have the tough hide and strength of an auroch. He was just a boy, just a helpless human boy. The realisation made him quiver.

"Scared, man-pup?"

"Go away," Gruffudd whispered. The wolves moved in with deliberate slowness, some laughing, others licking their lips. One leapt.

Gruffudd dove forward, rolling beneath the leaping wolf. He found himself in a flurry of limbs and snapping jaws. How he escaped the tangle, he could never figure out, but Gruffudd found his feet again and was running for all he was worth.

It wasn't enough. Growling and snarling, the wolf pack leapt after him, and they were swifter by far. Gruffudd screamed when the jaws of a wolf closed around his upper arm, the beast's forward momentum driving him to the ground. Another set of jaws closed around his ankle. Gruffudd screamed again as he was shaken roughly at both ends. The violent movement threatened to rend his shoulder from its socket. He squeezed his eyes shut.

Suddenly the jaws around his arm released, and a high-pitch yelp assaulted his ears. No sooner had that happened, than did the jaws about his ankle also let go. A deep, petrifying growl sounded near his left ear. Terrified, Gruffudd curled into himself, trying to hide his head with his arms.

There were higher growls now, and then the sounds of a terrible fight. Then more yelping and then everything went quiet. Gruffudd remained where he was, trembling, until a gentle tongue licked at his bleeding arm, accompanied by a worried whine.

Gruffudd snuck a peak from under his elbow and was relieved to see tall, thick limbs, still covered in ash but with black fur poking out here and there. He sprung up and threw his arms around the thick, ash-covered pelt at the hound's neck.

"Oh, Cysgod Mawr!" he sobbed. "I'm so sorry! I'm so sorry that I'm loud, and I'm useless and I can't hunt. I'm sorry!"

"Hush, pup," Cysgod Mawr replied gently. "I should not have lost my temper with you. It is not your fault. I forgot that man pups take longer to grow than my own kin. You are young yet. I shall just have to teach you how to hunt, that is all."

Gruffudd looked up in surprise. "But how? I don't have teeth or claws or anything!"

"Well, you shall just have to make yourself claws."

Gruffudd blinked in surprise. He remembered that his father often made blades out of black stone. 'Careful, boy,' he would say. 'These stones are sharper than the teeth any animal may possess.' Gruffudd had watched his father make the stones countless times. He probably could make his own claws.

"I will," Gruffudd whispered. "I will make my own claws. I'll make you proud of me, Cysgod Mawr."

The black hound chuckled. "I have no doubt. Come now. I have found a stream that is clean. You can clean that grime off you. Quickly now. The dead will attract the rocs, and a young man pup is just as easy a target as a dead wolf."

Gruffudd nodded. As the pair left the clearing, Gruffudd turned and saw three dead wolves lying amongst the trees, and the great shadow of a roc as the massive bird wheeled overhead. He shuddered.

Gruffudd did manage to make his claws. He also made spears and knives besides, and practised hard every day. Soon, no one could rival his skills with spear and knife. Cysgod Mawr taught him to hunt, her strategy adjusted to suit the abilities of a human. They became very successful, though the black hound would grumble about Gruffudd cooking the meat before eating his share.

Elk and wolf alike feared their approach. They roamed ever southward, forever away from the angry mountain that had forced them together. Though he had grown into a tall, broad man, Gruffudd never lost his taste for play, and he and Cysgod Mawr would chase and wrestle for amusement for hours on end.

One day, Gruffudd found a small lake and was bathing when a group of young women came, giggling as they walked to the water's edge. At first, Gruffudd tried to hide, unsure what to make of the sound that he had long ago forgotten. At first sight of the women he was captivated and forgot to hide.

The women seated themselves by the banks of the lake and were laughing as they played in the shallow water there. One girl spotted Gruffudd there and gasped. The others turned and soon Gruffudd was faced with half a dozen women and nowhere to hide. He froze on the spot.

One bold woman stepped forward, the white cloth she wore about her sticking to her skin where it had gotten wet.

"Hello," she said with a soft smile. A few of the other girls giggled.

Gruffudd tried to smile back, but was certain that it looked more like a grimace. The girls giggled again, and Gruffudd flushed in embarrassment. Unable to do anything else, he dove down into the water and swam away, coming up only when he was certain he was shielded from sight. There he remained, his heart pounding uncomfortably in his chest, until certain that the women had left. He rose from the water and went in search of his companion.

"Gruffudd," Cysgod Mawr greeted with a yawn. Gruffudd nodded and sat slowly down, distracted. Cysgod Mawr noticed and sat up.

"What is the matter?"

"I saw something at the lake."

"What did you see?"

"People."

The black hound felt an unexpected stab in her chest. She had feared this day more than any other – that her last remaining pup would leave her to join his own kind.

"They looked like me," Gruffudd was saying. "Only shaped..." Gruffudd struggled to find a description before giving up and simply drawing the image mid-air with both hands.

"What you saw were the females of your kind."

Gruffudd frowned. "I liked what I saw," he mumbled.

"Of course you did. You are supposed to."

"I don't know what that means."

Cysgod Mawr sighed. She licked Gruffudd on his cheek. "It means you are ready to join your own kind and have pups of your own."

Gruffudd studied Cysgod Mawr a while. "And you?"

"I am not a man," she replied. "I cannot be part of a man-pack."

"I am a man, you are part of my pack."

"That is different, Gruffudd."

"How?"

"It just is. Now sleep. We will find your pack in the morning."

Gruffudd was troubled by the sadness in the hound's voice, but he did not comment on it. Instead, he lay down beside the great dog and ran his hands through her thick pelt before falling into a troubled sleep.

Gruffudd awoke late that morning to find Cysgod Mawr watching him. He smiled at her. "Morning."

"You slept long."

"Yes."

"I have found where the man-pack has settled."

"Oh."

"You do not want to be with the females?"

"I do, but..."

Cysgod Mawr waited patiently in silence.

"...I don't want you to go away."

"I cannot stay. I have always known this time would come. Come, we'd best be off."

Cysgod Mawr rose and trotted away, and Gruffudd joined her. He could not help but be sad at the thought of leaving Cysgod Mawr. However, the excitement of seeing the women, of being amongst them was almost overpowering.

It took half a day of walking before the forest began to thin. The black hound stopped before a small rise.

"Over that rise is the encampment of the man-pack."

"Let's look," Gruffudd replied, unable to mask the excitement in his voice. Together, they crawled up the slope to the crest and peeked over. The small camp was a hive of activity.

Women sat near the fire, wearing skins of elk, and wildflowers braided into their hair. They were sewing and laughing together. Several men were there also, conferring by the fire, but apart from the women. In a crescent around the far side of the fire stood three round huts made of bowed wood and hide. A few children chased each other around them.

Gruffudd was mesmerised once more. He watched the scene with a smile on his face, and Cysgod Mawr watched him with a weight on her heart. Careful not to make any noise, she slinked down the slope and vanished into the trees.

"Are you certain that you will not come? I am sure they..."

Gruffudd's voice trailed off when he turned to speak to Cysgod Mawr and found her gone. He turned more and searched the line of trees. Of the black hound there was no sign. Tears stung Gruffudd's eyes.

"I love you, Cysgod Mawr," he whispered, hoping his sentiment would reach her though his words could not.

A sound caught Gruffudd's ear and he turned to see a spearhead pointed uncomfortably at his throat. Gruffudd followed the shaft of the spear until his eyes met that of an angry-looking man, dressed in skin trousers and boots and little else. Gruffudd's blue eyes widened in surprise and his mouth fell open.

"Who are you?" the man asked gruffly. It had been a long time since Gruffudd had heard human speech and he wasn't sure he could reply in kind. He blinked stupidly up at the man.

"Papa!" a breathless voice called. Gruffudd's eyes shifted to see a young woman running up the slope. It was the same young woman who had boldly greeted him at the lake. “Papa, wait! That’s him. That’s the boy I was telling you about.”

The man looked at his daughter, then at Gruffudd. “You’re naked,” he told the boy.

It had not mattered while Gruffudd was the pup of a black hound. Suddenly it was hugely important, and Gruffudd flushed with embarrassment.

“Wife!” the man shouted down the hill. “Bring some clothes. I’ve found a naked boy!”

Gruffudd could hear all sorts of laughing and excited chattering beyond the thick figure of the man, but could see nothing of what was actually happening. Before long, Gruffudd had been dressed and found himself sitting at the fire, dozens of faces turned expectantly towards him as he stumbled his way through his own story.

Miles away, Cysgod Mawr stopped her frantic run. She had been running north since she left her pup to the man pack. The pain in her heart had her running. If she slowed too much, it would return. Now she was too tired to run, and the exhaustion in her legs and the ache in her heart conspired together to buckle her legs. She lay in the thick carpet of leaves for a while, pining for the loss of her child.

The mighty black hound, Cysgod Mawr, last of her kind, might have died then and there of a broken heart if a familiar hungry yelp didn’t rouse her. The hound lifted her massive head and turned to spy a young wolf pup stumbling from its den towards her.

The tiny little thing yelped and pleaded for food as it made its awkward way forward. More pleading yelps from inside the den told Cysgod Mawr that there were five pups still inside; a handful for any mother. Cysgod rose and trotted over to the pup.

The scent lingering there of the adult mother was several days old.

“You poor little pup,” the Black Hound said gently. “Go back to your den. I will bring you a milking goat. Stay and hush. I will be back.” She picked up the pup and dropped it gently back into the den. “Stay,” she told all the pups inside. “Mama will be back soon.”

Gruffudd had been adopted into the tribe without much fuss. The tribesmen heard his story and agreed that he should be allowed to stay. He was given clothes and taught everything there was to know about being a man of the tribe. He learnt quickly, as he had done when Cysgod Mawr had taught him. He was even able to teach the men more efficient hunting strategies, strategies that Cysgod Mawr had described her pack using. For this, Gruffudd was given great status.

One thing disturbed the tribesmen though.

Gruffudd would spend hours after sunset, when everyone else was settling in to sleep, staring out over the plains, or into the woods, and listening. One evening, the daughter of the chief, the same girl who had first spoken to Gruffudd that fateful day at the lake, walked to his side.

"What are you looking and listening for?"

"Cysgod Mawr," he replied. "I miss her so"

"You should sleep, Gruffudd."

"In a moment, Aranhod. In a moment."

For five years, Gruffudd stood and listened and watched, and for five years he saw and heard nothing. He had all but given up hope of ever seeing Cysgod Mawr again. Then, one morning, a man screamed.

Gruffudd raced out of his tent to find the man by the fire, his spear at the ready. Gruffudd followed the man's line of sight and saw a pack of wolves slink back into the woods. Waiting until the last had crossed back into the thick trees, was the great black hound, her red eyes glistening bright in the morning sun.

Gruffudd smiled. At that precise moment, Cysgod Mawr caught sight of him, and her ears pricked forward.

"Cysgod Mawr!" Gruffudd called. The enormous black hound barked twice and turned, slipping back through the trees. Gruffudd laughed and hugged the frightened man by the fire. "She's alive!"

The man nodded dumbly and slipped away from Gruffudd, muttering under his breath.

That night, not too far away from the camp, Cysgod Mawr howled. Gruffudd heard and left the fire. He tilted his head up at the sky and howled in return. A chorus of howls answered. Some were Cysgod Mawr's and others her pack's. Gruffudd smiled. Each night was the same. In this way Cysgod Mawr and Gruffudd told each other every night that they loved one another.

In the difficult winters, when food was scarce, Gruffudd would leave some of a kill in the woods as a gift to Cysgod Mawr and her pack. More than once the tribe awoke to find a freshly killed carcass near their camp with wolf tracks scattered in the snow all around.

One spring, shortly after Gruffudd and Aranhod were wed, a terrible ruckus in the forest woke the camp. The noise was fearsome, and none save Gruffudd knew what it was. He had heard it many years ago as a frightened boy cowering before snarling wolves. A fight.

"No!" he cried. He grabbed his spear and ran into the woods. Aranhod gave a shout and followed. Before long, the entire tribe was chasing Gruffudd into the woods. They caught up with him just as he reached the clearing where the fight was taking place.

A young, large timber wolf had Cysgod Mawr's throat clamped tightly between his jaws. He shook her and the black hound yelped in pain. With a roar, Gruffudd cast his spear, impaling the wolf straight through. The wolf stumbled, then fell. With their leader gone, the invading wolves turned and fled.

Cysgod Mawr herself lay in a pool of her own blood. A high-pitched whine was all she could muster. Gruffudd ran to her side and fell to his knees.

"No," he whispered.

Cysgod Mawr wagged her thick black tail when she saw him – once, twice, then lost the strength for more.

"Cysgod Mawr," Gruffudd said, tears spilling out onto his cheeks. He reached out and stroked her head.

"Little pup," the black hound wheezed. "Do not weep. I am old now, and can lead the pack no longer. This has always been the way of things."

"But...."

"Hush now. Hush. I am well. I go to my kin. Gruffudd..."

Cysgod Mawr said no more. The light in her ruby eyes faded and her struggles fell still.

"Cysgod Mawr," Gruffudd said through his sobs. "I love you." He buried his face in her ruff and wept. When his weeping was done and Gruffudd raised his head, he found Cysgod Mawr's pack sitting in a semicircle around him.

"First pup," one wolf greeted. "I am called Brandun."

"I am honoured to meet you."

"Cysgod Mawr spoke very highly of you."

"Thank you."

"You were our friend in times of great need."

"As you were to me. I will always be your friend."

The wolf nodded. "And we will be yours. Our pack is your pack now Gruffudd, in honour of the noble hound who led us. We will be ever at your side, aiding you as you aided us, for however long this world shall last."

Gruffudd was silent for a long moment. "Thank you, Brandun. The children of Cysgod Mawr are a welcome addition to our tribe."

"Lead us Gruffudd, First Pup."

In this way did man and hound make the pact that have bound them ever since.

The Taming of Man II

It was many thousands of years after Cysgod Mawr and her First Pup, Gruffudd. In the north, the land was not forgiving, and so the men there still followed the old ways – hunting with their hounds.

In the southeast, men had begun to build permanent houses of stone. They learned to work the land for food and so no longer needed to follow the herds at change of season. In that land, in the territory of the great Kemi tribe, lived a young girl named Rhiannon.

She was a beautiful girl and, at aged six, was promised to the eldest son of the Chieftain. He was an old man when she was betrothed, and would be older still when it finally came time to marry him. Distraught and betrayed, Rhiannon fled her village. Where she went, no one knew.

Autumn followed summer, winter followed autumn. For ten winters Rhiannon was neither seen nor heard from, until, one summer, hunters stumbled across a large herd of wild horses. They saw Rhiannon, now a young woman and fully-grown. Naked as her birthing day, she ran with the horses as one of them. The hunters were filled with wonder.

They returned then to their great stone buildings and told their lords what they had seen. The lords went out to see it for themselves.

"Girl!" one lord called. "Come home to us, and submit to your lord."

She replied, "I chose my own lord!"

The men jeered and laughed and told her she was being foolish, and that the stallion could not be her lord for she was no filly. Rhiannon just laughed and claimed that she would sooner lie with the stallion than false lords of false caves, for she would lie with no one unless he was truly a lord.

The men grew angry and plotted to capture Rhiannon. The girl was as wild as the horses she ran with, and she was one of the herd. The stallion protected her fiercely and when one lord saw how well the stallion fought, he realised what power he would have if only he could ride it. He plotted to take the stallion for himself, for any man with that much power would be a lord over lords.

It took many weeks, but at last they caught the stallion and dragged him back. The lord of all horses, however, was as proud as he was powerful. He would not submit, no matter what cruelty men threw at him. The human lord fumed and raged until one of his men reminded him that he could be made a lord of lords – a true lord – if he had the girl lie with him. Then perhaps the stallion, lord of horses, would submit.

Evil thoughts grew in the mind of the greedy lord, and he declared to his best men that anyone who could capture the girl would be second only to him when he became a true lord. So it was that hunters from all over strove against one another to capture Rhiannon.

They soon discovered it would be no easy feat. Rhiannon was a wilding, and in her lived the spirit of all wild horses. She ran as fast as a horse, and was as strong as a horse, and as proud. All over the countryside did the lord's men chase Rhiannon. It was not until a well-aimed arrow hit her slender legs that they were able to capture her.

They took her to their lord. Rhiannon proved as proud as the mighty stallion and, try as he might, the lord could not get her to submit. She would not lie with him.

She kicked and screamed and bit until at last he threw her from his bed and declared, "If you think yourself a horse, then you will act as a horse ought before a lord! You shall carry every traveller who wishes to enter my home from the outer gate to the inner gate and when you are tired and spent, perhaps then you will lie with me."

"I will not lie with a man unless he is a true lord!' she replied.

The false lord was enraged. He had her lashed and chained to the inner gate of his keep with a chain that was as long as the road to the outer gate, and so she had no choice but to do as he told her, or else lie with him. For almost a month she carried men back and forth like a beast of burden. Her feet cracked and split and bled and her back ached until she could not stand upright.

One day, a tribesman from the west came dressed in simple leathers and furs. He stopped at the outer gate and greeted the girl as if she were more than a beast.

"Why are you chained and punished in this way?"

She told him everything, and how the brave stallion, the lord of all horses, was still tied in the stable, wasting away for want of freedom. The man was appalled.

"And who are you?" Rhiannon asked.

"I am called Kellan," the man replied. "Chief of my Clan on the plains beyond the mounds of the Old Ones where we live as the Old Ones did. I have come to trade furs and axes. Let me free you. Come back with me and I will protect you."

"I will go nowhere without my lord."

"Then I will free your lord."

Kellan entered the gate alone and on foot so that the lord of the false cave grew angry with Rhiannon and while he ranted and raved, the Chieftain stole the key to the girl's chains and then traded his wares as if nothing had happened. After, he stole into the stables and freed the stallion. The lord of horses bolted, running through both gates before an alarm could be raised.

In the confusion that followed, the chieftain managed to free Rhiannon and they ran towards the land of his clan. Kellan had not the spirit of wild horses, and could not run as fast as Rhiannon.

"Come," Rhiannon said. "Get onto my back, and I shall bear you home, as the lord of horses has borne me in times of great need."

Having not the time to argue, Kellan jumped on Rhiannon's back and she ran. The lord followed. In anger he loosed an arrow that pierced the girl's legs. In her stumble, Kellan was thrown from her back. The lord, who could not bear the thought of her declaring anyone lord but him loosed another arrow. It struck her in the chest.

The stallion had been watching from a safe distance. He screamed when Rhiannon was felled, and the jealous lord, who could not bear the thought of the stallion being lord in his lands, loosed his arrows upon him as well.

Kellan ran first to Rhiannon, who was barely alive.

"I will lie with no one who is not lord," she whispered. She died then in the chieftain's arms. The stallion approached, stumbling forward with many arrows in his mighty chest. At length, the chieftain rose and turned to him.

"My Lord, allow me to treat with you. If your herd becomes a part of my clan, I swear to keep them all safe from harm."

"That is well," said the stallion. "For my life bleeds from me swiftly and I will not be able to care for them myself."

The lord of horses called his herd to him and he told them of the pact he had forged with the chieftain.

"He is your lord now, and he will protect you as I have, and in return you must serve him as you have served me."

Then the stallion went to where Rhiannon lay. He lay down beside her and died, bled of his life.

Rhiannon and the lord of all horses were buried together in the mounds of the Old Ones. There, their spirits combined. The chieftain returned to his clan on the back of a horse, with the herd following, and his clan marvelled at the sight. From then on, herd and clan were one and the same, and to this day, the clans of the west walk with their horses as one of them.

Many summers later, Kellan met a lovely girl whom he could not deny. He wed her that very summer. After their hand fasting and the vows, the maiden leant towards the chieftain and said with a smile, "I will not lie with a man unless he is a true lord."

Keeper of the Wilds

Of all the old gods,
There remains but one,
To this day guard and custodian;
Keeper of the wilds.

Be warned, young fool,
His eyes are upon you,
Ever upon you as you trample through;
Keeper of the wilds.

Should you find a horn,
Blow upon it not, be warned.
Do not call him down, the old one;
Keeper of the wilds.

His hounds will track you,
His horse gives frantic chase,
And his arrows shall take you swift;
Keeper of the wilds.

Mind as you go,
As you walk in his woods.
Be wary of sinning against him;
Keeper of the wilds.

Harm not the trees,
Not nut, nor twig, nor leaves,
For his wrath is swift and sharp;
Keeper of the wilds.

Heed my words,
For I speak true,
Lest you become prey of The Hunt, and the
Keeper of the wilds.

River Woman

His name was Little Bear. The shaman gave the name to him after he killed a bear during his Man-Making. He once had a different name, but men weren't allowed to keep their boy names. As of now, Little Bear was a man amongst boys, and it was his job to watch the children and ensure that they were safe from harm. The children were playing now just a few feet from the mouth of the home cave, a safe distance from the cold river that flowed nearby.

It was usual for men of his ilk to take a wife or two immediately following their Man-Making. Little Bear, however, had never met any woman he might consider sharing his skins with for more than one night, and so had, shamefully, remained unmarried. He didn't care, though his mother certainly did. She would cluck disapprovingly at him and shake her head. Little Bear could only smile sadly in return.

In the distance, drumming started. There was to be a Woman-Making today, and all the women had gone away with the shamanka. Not too far away. It used to be that the women would travel a week out in order to initiate a new woman. It was terribly secret; more secret, even, than a Man-Making.

Things had changed. In the last few years, people starting going missing. Not just children, or the old, but strong men and women, who ought to know their way home. So many had gone, that getting lost couldn't be an explanation. Last year, the tribe had found the reason.

Other men, taller men, stranger men, had come to their lands, and they hunted the tribes here as if they were no more than animals. Hunted, and ate. Those that had gone missing had ended up in the bellies of the Tall Men. They were monsters, these men.

The tribes had always followed the herds at the change of season. Sometimes they would join the march of other tribes for a time, and share their food and stories. They had never expected to meet the Tall Men.

Meet them they did, however, one foggy day on their way to the autumn home. It had been a horrific and bloody clash. Even the women fought. Eventually, Little Bear's tribe had frightened off the attackers, or they considered this particular meal a little too hard in the earning. Either way, the Tall Men fled.

Little Bear had lost two half-brothers and his younger sister in that fight. The thought of it made his blood boil, even now, and his grip on his sturdy spear tightened until his knuckles turned white. He would have growled if he didn't think it would frighten the children.

Little Bear turned his head to the afternoon sun. It was lower in the sky than this time yesterday. Soon it would be time to move again, and it had the tribe on edge. They would, no doubt, meet the Tall Men again. Some of them had settled in lands nearby. Soon, Little Bear mused, the monsters would be fighting them for rights to the shelters too.

Good. Let them try.

Little Bear had debts to repay. He was unlike his kin in that sense. He angered quickly, and did not calm easily. And he remembered. Every good and every ill that was ever cast upon him, he remembered. He intended to make good on them all, one day.

A child screamed. Little Bear turned to see one of his charges topple over the edge of the sharply sloping hill that led straight into the frigid waters of the river. He shouted and chased the boy, but it was too late. The child landed in the water with a loud splash before Little Bear had reached halfway down the hill. Little Bear, like everyone else, could not swim.

Muttering a few choice curses, Little Bear altered his direction. He hoped to catch the boy before he went over the waterfall. So focused was he that he did not hear the splash further upstream. He did, however, see a figure gliding past, beneath the water's surface.

It was white like a fish, with pale brown hair that flowed behind like water weeds. It swam like a frog, but was undoubtedly shaped like a human; a Tall Man, slender and long of limb. Little Bear doubled his efforts. He would not let that monster reach the boy before he did.

It was of no use. Little Bear was running overland, and the Tall Man was in the water, swimming with the current. He lost sight of the fishy Tall Man and the boy in the white water that began a few feet before the waterfall. He searched for signs of the boy as he ran, praying to the ancestors that he would make it in time.

He didn't. Little Bear was frozen solid by the sight of the boy as he went head first over the water's edge. His heart missed several beats when, at the last minute, a slender white hand shot out of the water and grabbed the boy's ankle. The other hand reaching up out of the water to grasp the rough side of a mammoth-shaped rock that divided the waterfall in half.

Surprisingly strong for a creature so slender, the Tall Man hauled itself out of the water, still grasping the boy's ankle. Little Bear rejoiced at the sound of the boy's deep, gasping intake of air, even as Little Bear readied his spear.

Little Bear paused. The Tall Man was helping the boy up the rock. Moreover, for a Tall Man, it wasn't all that tall. When it turned to face him, Little Bear realised that this Tall Man was, in fact, a young woman. She looked at Little Bear with pale hazel eyes. The eyes were not monstrous, but rather sad, as she observed the readied spear.

The boy, coughing and spluttering and desiring comfort, reached out and wrapped the woman in a tight embrace. The woman held the boy, but never once took her eyes off Little Bear.

Little Bear slowly lowered his spear and the children caught up to him. One girl gasped and grabbed a hold of Little Bear's painted hide trousers in fear. One boy giggled, and another smiled and waved shyly. Little Bear hushed him, but that did not stop the strange woman from smiling and waving back, eliciting more giggles from the children.

"Are you alright, little one?" Little Bear called to the boy. The boy nodded, his head obstinately resting on the stranger's slender shoulder.

Little Bear nodded back and turned to the eldest of the boys. "Run and fetch my skins, rope, and bolas."

The boy nodded and ran.

"We're getting you a rope," Little Bear called. "Be brave now. We'll have you safe soon."

The boy whimpered and the woman stroked his wet head in a motion that was surprisingly gentle, for a monster. Little Bear narrowed his eyes at her, but could do nothing. It was not long until the eldest boy returned with the supplies. Little Bear grunted his thanks and tied the bolas to the rope.

"Catch!"

It was not the boy who caught the rope, it was the woman, and it was done with such a quick motion as to seem as if she had not moved at all. She tied the rope about her waist and stood. With a nod to Little Bear, she slowly leant her weight back. Understanding, Little Bear did the same. The boy clung to the woman's leg and began sobbing.

"You have to climb across," Little Bear called. The boy wailed and shook his head vigorously.

"Do it! Or I'll leave you on that rock!"

The boy's mouth fell open and he stared bug-eyed at Little Bear, who lifted his brows in response. Trembling, the boy stood, clutched the rope and looked up at the woman. She smiled at him. Steeling himself bravely the boy pulled himself up and began to shimmy across.

It was torturously slow. The boy's fingers were numbed by the cold, and he slipped more than once. Once over dry land, the boy simply let go, landing with a painful thump. The other children swarmed around him and the eldest wrapped him in a skin.

The woman on the rock watched with a smile before she began to untie herself. Little Bear frowned and tugged twice on the rope. She looked up, surprised. Little Bear tugged again and nodded. He always paid his debts, and he owed this woman a life. The woman walked forward and looked down at the frigid water, then glanced around.

There wasn't another way down. Unless she was willing to brave the steep drop of the waterfall, there was no way off the rock without help. The woman took a deep breath and dove into the water. The current caught her and she was over the edge, falling towards the cliff face.

Little Bear did not wait for her to reach the side. He began pulling immediately.

Below, the young woman struggled to haul her own weight up the rope. Like the child who went before her, the cold numbed her. It was not nearly as long as it felt before she was clinging to the edge, her feet scrambling uselessly to push her up. It was Little Bear who pulled her to safety, whereupon she fell unconscious into his arms.

Little Bear bundled the woman in skins and carried her to the home cave. The children followed. Once inside, Little Bear laid her down on his skins and started a small fire. Several of the girls began rubbing the stranger's smooth, pale skin in an effort to get blood moving again. Other girls were trying to dry her long hair.

Little Bear, useless when it came to healing, kept out of the way. He watched though, and found himself fascinated by the woman. Her skin was pale, so pale that it reminded him of quartz, and she was slender. Her limbs were long and her eyes large. She had no hair but for what was atop her head. This strange woman moved Little Bear.

The low, mournful note of a horn sounded. A hunting party had returned. Little Bear grimaced. He'd have some explaining to do. He looked over at the boy, who had gone to the woman's side and was now lovingly stroking her face. With a grumble, Little Bear stood and went to greet the party.

"Blessed to see you again," Little Bear said to Grey Elk, the elder who led the hunters. "I see you have brought rabbit."

"Blessed to see you again," Grey Elk replied, his brown eyes crinkling as he smiled at Little Bear. "We have brought rabbit. They are nice and plump too. Where are the children?"

"The children are inside. Grey Elk, there is something you should know."

"What is that?"

"There is a Tall Man here."

Grey Elk's smile fell and he lifted his spear. "Where? Where was he last sighted?"

Little Bear almost smiled. "He is a she. And she is inside the home cave, unconscious."

"You brought a Tall Man here?" Grey Elk was understandably furious.

"Grey Elk, please listen. One of the children fell into the river today. She saved him. She was alone. I could not leave her to die of the cold."

"The Tall Men are never alone! What if you've led them right to us?"

"If they were going to attack, they would have done it when it was just myself and the children. They would not wait until the home cave had its hunters again. She is quite alone."

That seemed to calm Grey Elk a little and he examined Little Bear a moment. "You are certain she is alone?"

"Yes."

Grey Elk grunted. "Let me see her, then. Take care of the rabbits," Grey Elk commanded his men. Curious, but unwilling to anger an elder, the hunting party remained outside. Grey Elk followed Little Bear to where his skins lay.

"There is no meat on her! And what of her bones? There seems to be little enough of that too!"

Little Bear shrugged. "Are not all Tall Men built so?"

Grey Elk shrugged. "They are not as broad as we. Even so, she is too skinny. Your mother will have to work to fatten her up."

Little Bear smiled slightly at Grey Elk's unvoiced acceptance. The rest of the tribe would take more convincing.

"I can accept her," he told Little Bear, "if what you say is true and she saved a child from drowning. But there are others that will need more convincing, Little Bear. She comes from a monstrous people."

"Perhaps she comes from a different kind of Tall Man. Surely if she was one of those evil men, she would not have saved a child's life?"

"I agree. Stick to reason, and don't get angry when facing the elders, or you will never win them over."

Little Bear nodded. "I know."

There was absolute mayhem when the other hunting parties returned. It took the elders a long while to silence the shouting and cursing. When at last silence fell, the elder Leaping Fox cleared his throat and looked at Little Bear.

"Explain yourself," he said.

Little Bear did just that and by the time his tale was over, everyone had fallen into ponderous silence. A length, Grey Elk cleared his throat.

"I believe that Little Bear is telling the truth, and that this Tall Man, at least, will not harm us."

"That may be so," Red Sparrow spat angrily. "But what of her kin when they find her here?"

A few others shouted their agreement.

"I am not sure she has kin," Little Bear replied.

"Of course she has kin!"

"If she did, why would she be travelling so far without them?" Little Bear countered. "Even the Tall Men travel in tribes. Would they have not come here by now?"

Leaping Fox cocked his head in thought. "That is a point."

"All the same, she cannot stay here," Charging Bison, Little Bear's father and chieftain of the tribe, grumbled.

"I can't very well cast her out into the night as she is," Little Bear snapped.

"No. You can wait until she is awake, then take her far away from here, and leave her there."

An angry wail from the back of the cave made everyone turn and the boy who had almost drowned was standing, glaring hard at Charging Bison. Charging Bison raised an eyebrow at Little Bear.

"The boy she saved," Little Bear said with a small smile. "It seems he wants her to stay also."

"Why do you want her to stay?" Red Sparrow asked, accusing.

Little Bear shrugged at him. "She saved the life of a child. She has no tribe. Casting her away would be to kill her. How can I repay the life of a child with cruel death?"

The council fell silent. At length, Leaping Fox sighed. "We will wait until the women get home. Then we'll see what is to be done."

With that, the council disbanded and everyone retired to their skins for the evening. Little Bear, his skins already occupied by the still-unconscious stranger and the boy she had saved, had no choice but to find a nearby patch of soft earth to sleep on. Come the morrow, the women would return and there would be another meeting.

It was mid-afternoon when the women returned. They were singing and giggling as they approached the home cave, and the newly made woman was at their centre, wreathed in summer blossoms of all kinds. The men were not smiling as they approached. Charging Bison's first wife, Skylark, didn't seem to mind.

She walked right up to her husband with a mischievous quirk of her mouth and sang as she threw petals all over the men. Charging Bison growled unpleasantly as he shook them off.

"Wife," he grunted. "There is an issue."

Skylark didn't care. She continued to sing and dance around the cluster of men, throwing petals. Laughing, the other women joined in, encircling the group and dancing around them until the new woman arrived. Then the singing stopped and the women parted, revealing the newly made woman in all her splendour.

"Husband," Skylark said, her brown eyes sparkling. "This is Walking Crow. She is a new woman. Is she not fine?"

"Indeed she is, wife," Charging Bison agreed. "Very lovely."

"Would you like a fourth wife?" Skylark jibed, poking Charging Bull in the ribs.

"What? And have my other three be jealous of her youth and beauty? I could not do that to them."

"You mean that you couldn't handle another wagging tongue," Red Sparrow muttered. Charging Bison simply grunted. Skylark laughed.

"You are so thoughtful, husband. Now, have you brought us a feast to celebrate?"

"We have."

"Oh good! Let's start cooking, then."

"First, wife, there is a matter we must discuss."

"Oh?"

Charging Bison took a deep breath. "Little Bear brought a Tall Man to the home cave," he said all in one breath, so that the words ran into one another.

The smile melted off Skylark's face. "What?" she asked, turning to Little Bear.

"She saved a child from drowning, and is without a tribe," Little Bear said.

Skylark remained silent, glaring at Little Bear with brown eyes that, once warm, were now hard and cold as flint. Little Bear shrank back a little.

"Oh, Little Bear!" Talking Badger, Little Bear's mother and third wife of the chief, said. "That was foolish."

"I owed her the life of a child," Little Bear replied defensively.

"Yes, and you always pay your debts," Charging Bison sighed. The chief turned to his third wife. "He's your son, wife," he said wearily.

"Please, Skylark," Little Bear said. "Come in and see her. She is such a tiny little thing. She couldn't hurt anyone."

The men who thought Little Bear a fool erupted into shouts again. Skylark put up a hand and all the men fell silent.

"I will see her."

That was something, at least. Little Bear led Skylark to where the woman lay asleep. The children had gathered there also, facing the entrance of the cave in a semi-circle around the stranger. The boy she had saved sat at the woman's head and was stroking her fine hair, hair that, once dried, was the colour of grass in the autumn dry.

"She is all bone," Skylark scoffed. She knelt and touched the girl's forehead. "Fever."

"The children tended to her after she came from the water and collapsed."

"She came from the water?"

Little Bear nodded. "To save a child from drowning."

"Tall Men eat children. Perhaps she is not a Tall Man at all."

"She's built like them. All limbs, and pale skin."

Skylark only grunted at this.

"What else would she be?"

"Perhaps she is a river spirit. I do not know. She is too small to be a Tall Man. Though she is young yet, so maybe she is." Skylark looked up at the boy. "She saved you, did she?"

The boy nodded gravely. Skylark sighed and looked up at Little Bear. "You are certain she has no kin?"

"Well, no," Little Bear admitted honestly. "But no one has come to claim her, and she was quite alone."

Skylark grunted again and stood. Without saying anything to Little Bear, she turned and walked back to the men and women who were waiting at the mouth of the cave expectantly. Little Bear trailed behind in apprehension. Skylark looked directly at Charging Bison.

"She stays."

That was that. No one argued with Skylark.

Charging Bison nodded. "Let's eat," he boomed. The women cheered and before long, the spoils of yesterday's hunt were roasting merrily. Little Bear approached Skylark during the festivities.

"Thank you."

Skylark smiled at him. "You have a soft heart, Little Bear, though you try to hide it. You are just like your father." She narrowed her eyes. "You would make a good husband for Walking Crow."

Little Bear flushed, but said nothing. He glanced back at the home cave before excusing himself to get more food. Skylark noted it, but said nothing as she turned back to the business of welcoming a new woman to the tribe.

It was sometime later when Skylark noticed Little Bear was missing. She beckoned Talking Badger over. "Little Bear has gone into the home cave to feed the river woman," Skylark told her. "Take some of the rabbit broth to him. He will not know that an empty stomach should not ingest roasted meat. Men are such fools."

Talking Badger smiled and did as she was told. She found Little Bear sitting beside the stranger with a platter of roasted meat. He was doing nothing, except sitting.

"Son?" Talking Badger touched Little Bear's shoulder. He blinked as if waking from a dream.

"Mother," he greeted with a smile.

"Here," Talking Badger said, handing Little Bear the wooden bowl of broth. "Roast meat isn't good for an empty stomach."

Little Bear nodded. Talking Badger sighed and sat down.

"River Woman," she said gently, shaking the stranger's shoulder. "Wake, River Woman. You must eat."

The woman stirred and her pale eyes fluttered open. She tried to push herself upright but found her arms unwilling. She fell down again and closed her eyes. This time it was Little Bear who shook her.

"River Woman," he said. "Wake. Wake, River Woman."

The girl opened her eyes again and, with Little Bear's help, she hauled herself into a sitting position. Blinking in the dim light, it took the girl a moment to realise that Talking Badger was there. The stranger tensed.

"It's alright," Talking Badger soothed. "I'm not going to hurt you, girl. Here. There is food." She pointed to the steaming bowl in Little Bear's lap. The stranger looked at Little Bear who nodded and smiled. He took up the crude wooden spoon filled with broth and held it to her lips.

"Cool it first, you fool!" Talking Badger snapped. "She'll burn herself."

Little Bear jerked the spoon back, spilling its contents on the floor. Talking Badger snatched the spoon from his hands, muttering, 'Men!' She took up more soup and, careful to cool it first, fed it to the stranger. The stranger ate almost the entire bowl before sleep began to overtake her again. She struggled against it; there was something she wanted to know. She placed her palm on Little Bear's chest and looked up at him with questions in her eyes. Little Bear frowned, not understanding.

Talking Badger did. "Little Bear," she said gently. Understanding flowed into Little Bear's eyes. He nodded and touched his own chest.

"Little Bear," he repeated. Then he placed both hands on his mother's shoulder. "Mother," he said.

The stranger looked over at the woman and smiled. Talking Badger turned to Little Bear. "You just introduced the woman who is sleeping in your skins as 'mother.' Does this mean you are married?"

Little Bear's face flushed bright pink and Talking Badger smiled. She pressed her hand against her chest and said, "Mother." It was better, after all, that Little Bear be married to the stranger, than to remain so shamefully unmarried. Little Bear blinked at his mother in surprise before turning back to the stranger and finding that she was almost asleep where she sat. With a sigh, he lowered her down again.

"There now," Talking Badger soothed, covering the stranger's tiny frame in skins. "Sleep well." She looked at Little Bear. "Come on, back to the fires."

With a sigh, Little Bear did as he was told. When Talking Badger returned to the fire, she went to Skylark. "He wants to marry her," she told the head wife. Skylark smiled at her.

"I know."

It was another two days of careful attention from Little Bear and his mother before the stranger was able to walk around, and an entire week for her fever to break. Though at first there had been a great deal of suspicion, by the time River Woman could walk unassisted, most everyone had gotten used to her unusual form wandering ghostly pale about the caves.

They had also gotten used to calling her River Woman, and all agreed that it could not be certain that she was a Tall Man. After all, the Tall Men were tall, and she was rather short. It became widely believed that she was, in fact, a river spirit.

River Woman did not speak, but was able to make her thoughts known by using her hands and eyes. It had taken the tribe several weeks to figure out just what her hands were saying. She also did things very differently from the women of the tribe. She weaved her baskets oddly, and did not know how to scrape and cure skins for clothing.

She did, however, know the water very well, and caught many fish to eat. The tribe had not eaten fish before River Woman had arrived, and many did not like it. Skylark and Charging Bison adored it. Little Bear could tolerate it, and he would eat it often just to see River Woman happy.

River Woman was often left in the home cave alone. She would wander through the tunnels as far back as they would take her. Little Bear found her one day in the Cavern of Memories, a small fish oil lamp in her hands. She was gazing at the many paintings that spanned through the cavern. One scene in particular had her attention – fearsome Tall Men hunting tribesmen with cruel spears.

Little Bear joined her silently. At length, she turned to him with eyes that asked a thousand questions. Little Bear sighed. He pointed to a Tall Man on the wall. "You," he said, pointing at her. Then he pointed to a tribesman with a spear through him. "Us," he said indicating himself.

River Woman's eyes went wide and her hands flew up to her mouth. She went further along the wall to where an image of a tribesman was being eaten. She pointed to the dismembered man, and then to Little Bear. Little Bear nodded sadly. This time, River Woman's eyes filled with tears. She shook her head, and using her hands, indicated that she ate only fish, and had never eaten any tribesmen.

Little Bear smiled and brushed the tears away. He chanced a kiss on her cheek and was pleased when she smiled shyly. He kissed her on the mouth. She did not resist. Pleased, Little Bear pulled her close and, in the Cavern of Memories, he made River Woman his wife.

River Woman lived very happily with Little Bear and his tribe for many years. She had become Little Bear's sun and moon. He would hold her close every night by the fire, and seemed entirely uninterested in taking a second wife. Not one year into their marriage, River Woman had given Little Bear a beautiful baby boy. The boy had his mother's pale eyes, but his father's build and shock of dark auburn hair. They called him Laughing Cub, because he liked to laugh, and would do so often and loudly.

River Woman would make strange sounds at the boy, who would repeat them back to her. This seemed to make her happy, so no one cared overmuch. Life was good.

Things changed abruptly during the spring trek, when the tribe left the winter home to return to the home cave.

They chanced across a wandering group of Tall Men, and the Tall Men were on the hunt. There was little warning – a shout from Grey Elk and suddenly spears were flying. Little Bear was struck in the hip, falling to the ground with a grunt of pain. River Woman screamed and ran to him. Neither Skylark nor Talking Badger could stop her.

One of the Tall Men caught her and hauled her aside. He had a flint knife to her throat before he realised she was not one of the tribesmen. He shouted to his hunters and they withdrew, taking River Woman with them.

River Woman struggled hard against the man as her child screamed for her.

"Mama! Mama!" he screamed, tears streaming down his chubby young cheeks. The tribe watched in helpless silence as River Woman was dragged away. Only when the Tall Men had vanished did Talking Badger dare break the protective circle and run to her son's side.

"Little Bear! Little Bear!" she cried, shaking him back into consciousness. Little Bear groaned and, grasping the spear with bloodied hands, ripped it from his hip with a roar. He sat up and looked around.

"Wife!" he shouted when he did not see her. "Wife!"

Talking Badger started sobbing. "The Tall Men have taken her."

Little Bear sat in stunned silence for a moment. Then his temper boiled over. With a snarl, he clawed his way to his feet and marched over to the tribe. He picked up some spears, and all the weapons he owned.

"What are you going to do?" Charging Bison asked his son.

"I'm going to get her back," Little Bear growled.

"Papa?" Laughing Cub asked in the nonsensical sounds taught by River Woman. Little Bear stroked this son's head and kissed him on his brow.

"You must be strong, son. Father is going to go find mother. I'll bring her back. I promise."

"You are wounded," Skylark pointed out. "You will be weak when you face them."

"I will not let them eat my wife!" Little Bear snapped.

Skylark turned imploring eyes to her husband, but Charging Bison did not stop his son. Little Bear was as stubborn as his namesake when his blood was hot. The tribe wailed in grief as Little Bear left them and followed the tracks of the Tall Men, and none so loud as Laughing Cub.

For three days, Little Bear pursued the Tall Men. Through plains and woods, and over hills he chased them, until, one evening, he spied a small fire and heard their harsh, barking laughter. He crept forward, certain that River Woman was alive. If they had eaten her, he would have found the bones.

Little Bear spied River Woman kneeling by the fire, her hands bound with grass rope and her face muddied and streaked with tears. The Tall Men were chattering at her and pushing her around and laughing. It was too much for Little Bear. With a roar, he rose to his feet, and charged into the camp.

Skylark had spoken true. Three days of continual running and the wound at his hip weakened Little Bear considerably. He was fighting five Tall Men. He knew he could not win. He was surprised to still be standing after killing two. A glancing blow to the side of his head by a club brought him to his knees, his vision swimming.

River Woman screamed

Little Bear expected the deathblow to follow. It never did. Gathering himself, he turned around to find River Woman standing over the body of the Tall Man who had struck him, a bloodied flint knife in her hand. She was glaring at the two remaining Tall Men, the fire turning her pale eyes a devilish red.

The Tall Men hesitated before one grinned. He made sounds at River Woman, sounds that Little Bear realised were supposed to be speech. The woman replied in kind, and one of the men laughed, pointing at Little Bear. The River Woman nodded and the laughter died away to expressions of disbelief.

Whatever River Woman told the Tall Men, it made them angry. One drew a knife from his belt and lunged at River Woman. Little Bear lurched forward, but too late. The Tall Man had plunged his knife into River Woman's belly and Little Bear's crashing weight served to do nothing but throw the man sideways after the fact.

The sight of River Woman's blood sent Little Bear into a rage such as never before. Rage lent him strength, and Little Bear once again lifted his spear. He fought hard. The long-limbed Tall Men had not a chance, for the spirit of the bear had woken in him.

It was over before the sun had finished setting. The two remaining Tall Men were dead in the grass, Little Bear standing over them, growling. The growl turned into a wail when he saw River Woman, her blood soaking into the thirsty ground.

"River Woman," he sobbed. "Wife?" He shook her, but her large eyes did not open. Little Bear keened by her side until he had no more strength for tears. He lifted her in his thick arms and stumbled towards the home cave.

It was a week before he arrived, drenched and shuddering from the spring snows. He clung to River Woman and placed one numb foot after another until he heard someone shout his name. He had been so disoriented by grief and nearly blind by the thick drifts that he did not realise that he had reached the home cave and very nearly walked past it.

Charging Bison ran out into the snows to him. "Little Bear!" Then he saw River Woman, almost dead in Little Bear's arms. "Oh no," he breathed.

Little Bear almost collapsed then. If it were not for the strength of his father, and the many hands that had come to help, Little Bear would never have made it inside. He lost consciousness shortly after.

Little Bear was unconscious for the entire spring. It was summer before he opened his eyes.

River Woman seemed trapped between life and death and remained there until the day before Little Bear's eyes opened. On that day, she breathed her last shuddering breath.

It was Little Bear who discovered it. He had rolled over and opened his eyes to find his wife lying beside him. He had reached out to touch her pale face only to find it cold. His anguished wail woke the cave.

They did not bury River Woman inside the cave, as they would have done for one of their own. She came from the river, and it was to the river they returned her. Little Bear carried her in himself. He waded in until the water was around his chest. His shoulders shaking from grief, he released River Woman. The current took her then, and she floated downstream a while, before the water embraced her fully and she was swallowed.

"Little Bear," said Talking Badger gently. "Come."

Little Bear turned to her, his brown eyes blank. He looked upon his son, then up at Charging Bison who held the boy.

"Look after him," Little Bear said. Then he let his legs go, and the freezing water closed over his head.

"Little Bear!" Talking Badger screamed.

Charging Bull said, "He is gone to be with his wife. Let him go," even as tears streamed down his brown cheeks.

"Papa?" queried Laughing Cub.

The tribesmen turned as one and returned to the home cave to mourn. All save Talking Badger. She stayed by the river's edge, watching in case her son should surface again. At sunset, Skylark collected her and guided her home. Little Bear was never seen again.

To this day, tribesmen gather around their fires to hear the tale of River Woman, and young men are warned: dare not go near the water, lest a spirit steal your heart, and drown you.

The Dying God

"Stop! Thief!" the baker hollered as the girl shot down the street. She tucked the loaf of bread, still warm from the ovens, close to her tiny, underfed frame as she dodged around merchant and patron alike in the market.

Shouts rumbled through the crowd, and bodies started pressing in on her, hands reaching out to grab her. The baker's two sons had given chase and were gaining, fast. Scrawny though she might be, the girl was clever and she spun and weaved like a dancer as she moved effortlessly through the crowd. Until...

Crash!

The sound was deafening to her as she flew bodily into a captain of the city guard. The force of the impact threw her backward. She landed painfully onto her back. The wind was knocked violently from her lungs as she landed.

Blinking to rid her eyes of the glare and dust, it took the girl a moment to realise that someone had grabbed her by her elbow and was hauling her to her feet.

"Alright, you," a gruff voice said amidst the rustle of wool and steel. "Up you get."

The girl looked up as she found her footing. The captain scowled down at her.

"Give me that!" he snapped, yanking the loaf of bread from her arm. Devoid of its warmth, the girl began to shiver. The trembling did not stop as the guardsman pulled her back to the baker. He gave her a shake as he presented her to the angry merchant.

"Here's your bread," the captain said, handing the now-dusty loaf to the red-faced baker, who glared hard at the girl. She returned the glare with an impertinent gaze of her own.

"Miserable wretch," the baker muttered darkly at her. He spoke next to the captain. "Throw her in the dungeon like the rest of the miserable street rats. Let's see her steal a man's living from in there."

The girl scowled. Noting that the captain had forgotten to put on his leather gloves, she twisted and bit down hard on his thumb. Roaring in pain, the guardsman released her. Swift as a swallow, the girl spun and vanished into the crowd. The captain cursed and gave chase.

Desperate to avoid gaol, the girl took a turn most avoided and found herself sprinting full tilt down a derelict alley towards the run-down house that sat quiet and dark at the end of it.

Some said the house existed before the city was built. It was haunted, they said, a place where ghosts and ghouls roamed the halls. Evil rites once took place there, they said. So afraid of this place were the citizens of the city that no windows faced it, no doors opened on the streets that surrounded it and no one, not one, dared to approach it.

The girl paused a moment before the sound of the captain and his men huffing behind her spurred her forward once more. That house had to be better than rotting away in some damp, dark cell in the middle of town.

"Stop!" the captain called from the top of the alley. "Stop you foolish child!"

The girl would not stop. She ran on until she reached the corroded green gates. The gates themselves were thick, heavy, and locked. However, the hinges had rusted away, and the stone that supported such heavy doors had crumbled, leaving a small gap between the tall, thick walls that surrounded the house, and the tall thick gates that marked the entrance. She squeezed into the gap and vanished from sight.

"Stupid, stupid girl," the captain muttered, when he reached the gate. He dared not enter that yard. Then he grinned. One night in that house, and she will have wished she had gone to gaol instead. With a shrug, the captain turned to his men.

"We post guards at the gate in case the girl tries to get back out. She'll wish for gaol in the morning."

The guardsmen laughed gruffly.

The girl wasn't quite sure what to have expected in the front garden of a haunted house, but she did not expect this. The garden, now overgrown and unkempt, had clearly once been beautifully designed.

Tall wooden carvings stood as silent sentinels beside taller, broad trees that spread their canopies over the paved, weed-strewn path to the house. Several of the trees were in full bloom, and yellow and purple blossoms scattered over the pale pink stones of the pavement.

Though the wooden statues were rotted and crumbling, some of their features could still be seen. One was of a bearded man, and etched in relief on his side was a fearsome-looking boar. Another was simply a tall post etched with symbols and markings that the girl could not quite make out. The yard itself was quite expansive, with many trees and, the girl just noticed, a small circle of shoulder-height standing stones.

It was not at all like a haunted scene ought to be. It was mid-morning, and the sun was shining, obscured only by the occasional scuttling white cloud. Birds were singing lustily from the shrubs and trees in the yard. Two grey squirrels chased each other, chattering away like crones at a loom. A rabbit chewed lazily on a dandelion as it watched the girl, quite unafraid.

The street urchin turned her attention to the house. It must have been grand once. Tall green doors, marked with strange swirls and symbols stood silent and strong at the front of the house. There were no windows that faced into the front garden. There was only the enormous pair of doors set into the same grey-green stone as the garden walls.

Chilled by the wind and lack of food, the girl walked cautiously down the path to the doors. She touched them and found them cold as steel. "Bronze," she whispered to herself. The garden gates must have been made of bronze as well, turned green by decay.

Gates in the wealthiest parts of the city were usually made of iron and, with the exception of the patterning on the bronze doors, they differed little in appearance to the ones this house possessed. Perhaps this house was as old as the tales said, older even than the knowledge of iron. That seemed impossibly old to the eight-year-old street urchin.

She could hear guards talking at the gate. Jesting cruelly about how long she might last in this terrible place. She turned back to the garden. There had to be another route of escape; a tree close to the wall, perhaps, or a stone high enough to let her climb over the wall. She could find no such thing, though not for lack of trying.

Hunger plagued the girl, so, biting her lip, she turned back to the large doors. Spying a large brass ring on the door, she reached up and took it. Heaving with all her might, she pulled. Nothing happened. The girl scowled and tried again. Her feet scrambled on the gravel-strewn paving stones as she dragged her weight forward, but failed to open the door.

In frustration, she kicked the door, and hurt her toe. Uttering a few choice curses under her breath, the girl tried once more. Nothing. She pounded at the door with a small fist.

"Hello?" she called into the empty air as she pounded. "Please. Hello? Let me in. It's cold. I'm hungry. Please?"

There was no answer. That house had been deserted and derelict hundreds of years before she was born. Giving the door one last spiteful kick, the girl wandered back into the sunlight and sat down to sulk.

She was not always a street girl. In fact, she belonged to a noble family; *the* noble family, as it were. Her father had been an earl, and the red fox was his sigil. Their castle stood just on the outer edge of the city. It was now occupied, however, by someone else.

It had all happened such a long time ago, she could barely remember it. There had been a war. Her father had gone. So had the king. Her father came back. The king did not. That started another war. People had to choose sides. Her father chose the side that lost, and the winners came in the dead of the night to ensure he never chose again.

Traitor. That's what they called him. The penalty for treason was death. The fighting broke out first in the courtyard, with such tumult as to wake the rest of the house. Her mother had come into her room carrying the clothes of a servant girl. Before she knew it, the once daughter of an earl was disguised and given into the care of the household staff. Before her tearful mother kissed her goodbye, she removed her ring and gave it to her only daughter.

"Keep it safe, my love," she had said. "I will come looking for you. I promise."

Then she was gone, vanishing in a rustle of silk to stand by her husband's side as the enemy came streaming in.

"I am the king's man!" she heard her father roar as the enemy soldiers burst into the hall. Then her mother screamed and her father stopped bellowing. She, herself, saw nothing as she ran down the castle halls, sobbing in fear.

The soldiers had managed to capture the group she was with, but a brave act by one of the young laundresses, an act that earned her a dagger in the stomach, set the young noble girl, and several other children, free. They disappeared into the night and melted into the city streets.

She had heard later that the entire noble family had been executed. Her father beheaded in his hall, his two sons dying in the fight. The good lady, they said, had been burnt at the stake for a witch. When she had politely enquired why, they told her it was because she had red hair, and all redheaded women were obviously witches.

Tears stung the girl's eyes as she recalled that terrible night, and the horrors of life afterwards. No one expected a noble born to be a petty street thief and, coupled with the emaciating effect of constant hunger and the grime that turned her red hair dull brown, she was safe from recognition. That didn't ease the life any.

The girl curled up on the pavement, wrapping her arms around her stomach in a bid to stop the hunger pangs. It did not work. She stared blankly at the falling blossoms ahead of her, its strange beauty now lost on her. She had moved too much today, and had her meal taken from her for it. The hunger was making her nauseous. So nauseous, in fact, that she almost missed the popping, grinding noise behind her. It rang through the crisp air with a sound that was both bright and ominous.

Uncurling herself, despite the pain, the girl looked behind her. One of the enormous brass doors now stood ajar. Frowning, and almost able to forget her hunger, the girl stood and walked cautiously to the door. The crack was still too small to squeeze through, so she took a hold of the bronze ring once more and heaved with what little strength she had left. Reluctantly, the door opened wider. She squirmed through and found herself enveloped in darkness.

"Hello?" she called into the cavernous black before her. There was no echo. Here, despite the darkness, it was warm, and it smelled strangely familiar. She looked down. The little sliver of light that worked its way in from outside highlighted a faded rug on a dark granite floor. It was a design she was wholly unfamiliar with. She stepped forward one timid step.

"Hello?" she called again. The door creaked behind her and slammed shut. The darkness was now complete. Frozen in place by fear, the girl stood and trembled.

"Come closer, child," a soft, deep voice rumbled from somewhere ahead. The girl quailed.

"Do not fear," the voice said gently, the words touched at the edges by a smile. "I shall not harm you."

Still afraid, but finding her curiosity a stronger force, the girl edged forward. Then stopped.

"Well now, you are but an infant," the voice said.

"Who are you?"

"I have many names, child. Some are less flattering than others. Which one would you like to have?"

"Well, what name did your mother give you?" She could almost feel the man's smile in the darkness.

"That is too old to be uttered now. You may call me Hunter, if it pleases you."

"I suppose I shall have to, since it is the only thing I know to call you."

There was a deep rumbling sound that may have been laughter.

"I can't see anything," the girl said.

"Of course. Where are my manners?" There was a gentle hissing sound and then a golden light that grew slowly from candles dotted all over. The light grew to reveal an enormous room with bookshelves that were two stories high. The second story of books was bordered by a narrow landing that ran all the way around the room. A spiral staircase led to the landing on the far wall of the enormous room.

The girl's eyes widened to the size of dinner platters and she gasped. Her father had collected books also, but his library was not nearly this size. She wandered forward into the centre of the room, taking in the sight and smell of the books with delight before she noticed that she could not see the owner of the voice.

"Where are you?"

"Here," the voice said from behind the girl. She spun on her heels and stared. Sitting on a dark obsidian chair that was so large it was almost a throne, was a tall man. He was taller than any man she had ever seen, with broad shoulders. His face, however, was hidden beneath the hood of a long, black cloak.

"What is your name, child?" he asked as he closed the massive tome he was holding.

The girl hesitated. What if this man was one of the enemy, one of the many servants of the new earl? The name of the youngest child of the old earl was not common, and identifying herself with it could spell trouble. Yet, he did not wear the sigils of the new earl. His clothing seemed ragged, like the men who spent their time in the wilds. His hands, the only uncovered part of him, were free of the jewels that noblemen were wont to wear. She decided to risk it.

"Sinopa."

The man cocked his head to the side and smiled, or, at least, she imagined he smiled. "Sinopa. That is an old name also, and rare."

"I was named for my great grandmother," she answered truthfully. She silently chastised herself. If he had any doubts about who she was before, she just confirmed it for him. He seemed less interested in this than she would have guessed.

"Well, Sinopa," he said pleasantly. "It has been a long, long time since I have had guests. Welcome. Are you hungry?"

"Yes," Sinopa breathed, her stomach clenching at the prospect of once again having something other than itself to devour.

"Then come." The man stood lithely and held out his hand. "I will have a meal prepared for you."

Hesitantly, Sinopa took his hand. It was warm and dry and rough, like her father's hands had been. Tears stung Sinopa's eyes at the sudden memory, tears she blinked away furiously. The man looked down at her.

"You should wash first," he noted.

Sinopa was starving, and bathing was the last thing on her mind. All the same, she did not wish to insult or anger her host. She sighed and said, "Mother said it isn't proper to go to the table unwashed."

"Your mother is a wise woman. Very well, I shall find you a chamber suitable for sleeping, and have a bath prepared for you."

"Thank you."

They walked together in silence down a hall, the entrance to which was directly to the right of the thick bronze doors.

"You have many books," Sinopa noted.

"Yes. It has become a pastime for me."

"Have you read all of them?"

"Yes. Several times over."

"Really? That must have taken forever!"

The man who called himself Hunter rumbled his deep laughter, but said nothing.

"My father used to collect books," Sinopa noted. She fell into silence. After a time, Hunter spoke.

"Do you read?"

Sinopa shook her head. "I had started to learn, but...."

"But?"

"I stopped." Sinopa clamped her lips together. She was being altogether too loose with her information, and that could get her killed.

"That will not do. I can teach you, if you like."

Sinopa stopped dead. "Would you?"

"I do not offer unless I intend to fulfil it. I will teach you."

"Oh, thank you!"

Hunter smiled, or so it seemed, then stopped. Sinopa looked around her. She realised that they had been walking downhill for a time, and that the constructed grey stone gave way to smoothed pinkish stone that looked as if it had been carved rather than built. Before her the tunnel echoed on in darkness, while behind her torches flickered with smokeless flame. She had not seen anyone before them, and definitely knew that they had not stopped to light those torches. She greatly wondered how it was that they were now lit.

Hunter pushed on a wooden door to his left and it swung open soundlessly. He walked in, taking Sinopa with him. As soon as he entered the room, the fireplace sprung to life and a large bedchamber was revealed, with a large, very comfortable-looking bed situated pleasantly before the fireplace.

"Oh my!" Sinopa breathed. "A real bed!"

"Is it not to your liking?"

"Oh, no, no, no. This is wonderful! Thank you!"

"A little plain, perhaps. I shall have a tapestry brought in. The bathing room is through there," Hunter said, pointing at a roughly semicircular opening in the right wall. "I will await you in the dining hall. Do not fear getting lost, the way will be lit."

"Thank you," Sinopa replied, still staring about her with wide eyes. Nodding, but saying nothing, the hooded man named Hunter quietly left Sinopa in the bedchamber.

Sinopa wandered through the opening as if in a dream. No sooner had she stepped into the bathing room, than flames jumped up from the candles and lit a large brass bathtub filled with steaming fresh water. On a table beside the tub sat vials of scented soaps and creams. Hanging on a rail on one of the ends of that table, a thick towel and bathrobe.

Sinopa hurriedly tore the rags she wore from herself, and even took the pouch containing her mother's ring from around her neck. She stepped into the tub, feeling herself relax as the warm water covered her. The tub was so big she could almost go swimming in it. For the first time in many, many months, Sinopa scrubbed herself clean and even washed her hair, restoring the deep red of her locks that identified her as her mother's daughter.

Satisfied that she was clean enough to appear presentable at dinner, Sinopa hauled herself out of the tub and dried off. Throwing the robe around her, she wandered back into her room, to find a tapestry now hanging from the wall, a richly embroidered brown gown laid out on the bed and matching slippers on the floor beside it. It was a little large for her, but not so much that it would fall off. She might just trip over it, however.

With the promise of food wafting in through the tunnel, Sinopa left the room and began walking. The way had indeed been lit, each turn marked with light, while other offshoots of the tunnel remained dark and mysterious.

Even still, Sinopa followed her nose more than the light of the torches and soon found herself standing beneath the tall, carved ceiling of the dining hall. The hall was expansive, containing row upon row of tables and benches, all of which sat empty. At the far end of the hall, on a raised platform stood a long table, with cushioned chairs facing the entrance. At the middle of the table, beside the largest of the chairs stood Hunter.

The table was laid with what most nobles would call a modest supper. A leg of roasted boar sat in the centre, with a small bowl of nut sauce beside it. A wooden bowl filled with steamed wheat, a plate with a large circle of dark bread, a platter of vegetables fried lightly in butter and a bowl of apples stacked neatly also sat expectantly on the table. To Sinopa, it seemed a feast and she felt she might faint at the sight of it. It was all she could do not the run to the head table.

She gratefully accepted the chair Hunter offered her and sat down, unable to keep her eyes off the food. Hunter served her himself, giving her just a little bit of everything. It had been a long time since Sinopa's stomach had tasted food, and it would not take well to too much.

"Eat slowly," he warned as he placed the platter before her and began to fill his own plate. Though Sinopa was sorely tempted, she had not forgotten the manners her mother had taught her, and did not touch her cutlery until her host did. Hunter noted it with little more than a half-smile.

No sooner had she placed the first mouthful of food on her fork than three enormous black dogs came bounding up the hall, their tongues lolling happily from their mouths. Upon sighting Sinopa, all three stopped and turned their wolfish heads in her direction, their ears pricked forward. Sinopa stopped eating in shock as she realised that their large eyes glinted red in the light of the hall.

"My hounds," Hunter said quietly to Sinopa. "Do not fear them. They will not harm you."

"What manner of dogs are they?" Sinopa whispered back. "They look like giant wolves."

"An old breed," Hunter replied. "One no longer seen much, except in the north, across the sea."

Hunter whistled, and the hounds forgot Sinopa and continued their happy run to their master's side. All three milled about the table as Hunter momentarily forgot his supper and greeted his hounds with affectionate mussing of their ruffs.

One at a time, and still in a frenzied happiness, they sniffed at Sinopa and, apparently finding her agreeable, promptly ignored her for their master's affections. Sinopa couldn't help but smile as the mysterious, hooded man seemed to forget himself a moment and play with his dogs.

When, at last they had calmed down, Hunter returned to his meal and so too did Sinopa. He ate slowly and deliberately, forcing Sinopa to do the same so as not to seem rude. It was well that she did, for she had barely begun to eat before she felt full. It was delicious, and Sinopa refused to leave any food left on her plate.

"Are you still hungry?" Hunter asked her.

Sinopa shook her head. "Though I wish I was. That was delicious."

Hunter smiled.

"It seems that you were expecting more people," Sinopa ventured. She waved her hand around to indicate the rows of tables and benches. Hunter grunted.

"There was a time, a very long time ago, when I housed and taught many people. They lived here with me, tended to the garden in the front, and the crops in the back. They would go into the world outside, and sell any spare food we had, and teach others. Every year from every corner of this island, people would flock to the gates, hoping to be selected to live in this house."

"Where did they all go?"

Hunter shrugged. "Something changed in the world," he said vaguely. "And fewer and fewer people came to my doors. And then, no one came. Not for many, many years. All those who lived with me here grew old and died. All except one."

"Who?"

"Her name is Mirja. She came from across the sea with her brother. Only she was accepted. She is very old now, and cannot come dine with me here." There was a deep sadness to Hunter's voice and Sinopa felt sorry for him.

"It must be lonely."

Hunter nodded. "Yes. And when she is gone, for go she must, I will have no use for this house. All the books I collected..." Hunter spoke no more and Sinopa looked down at her plate in silence.

"I would like to meet Mirja," Sinopa said at last.

Hunter smiled sadly and nodded. "When I am done, I will be taking her evening meal to her. You are welcome to accompany me. No doubt she will rejoice at your presence."

"I should like that very much."

"That is well."

Sinopa remained in silence as Hunter finished his meal. She was approached by one of his hounds, who sniffed at her with interest. Timidly, Sinopa stroked the dog's massive head, and earned herself a wet lick. She giggled.

"Cabal likes you," Hunter noted. "That is a good sign."

Sinopa smiled at Hunter briefly before turning her attention back to the dog. It was not much longer before Hunter stood and, taking a small plate of food with him, walked with Sinopa through the tunnels. Stopping at a door, Hunter rapped politely.

"Enter," a voice rasped. Hunter pushed on the door and the hounds rushed forward, greeting an old woman dressed in a brown robe with the same frenzied joy with which they had greeted Hunter. Mirja had hardly any time to put down her embroidery before the dogs were upon her. She laughed and stretched out arthritic hands to play with them.

"Down," Hunter said gently and the hounds backed away, their tails wagging furiously. Hunter entered and Sinopa trailed behind. Mirja did not notice the girl until Hunter bent to place the food on the table where Mirja sat and kiss the old woman on the cheek.

"Why!" Mirja exclaimed. "Who is this?"

"Mirja, this is Sinopa. She arrived this morning."

Mirja clapped her hands together as her weathered face changed to an expression of sheer joy. "Another acolyte!" she breathed. "At long last, another one!" She held out both hands and Sinopa took them, a little confused. They felt like paper, but still pleasant. Hunter scowled.

"I am not accepting any more acolytes. She is a guest, nothing more."

"Oh heavens," Mirja said, waving at Hunter dismissively. "But of course you are."

Sinopa snuck a glance at Hunter, who was now emanating an air of annoyance. Mirja seemed to pay his mood no heed. "Oh child, you are too skinny. Have you eaten?"

"Yes," Sinopa replied.

"Not enough clearly. Are you not feeding your guests now, my Lord?" Mirja demanded of Hunter.

My Lord? Sinopa turned and looked in surprise at Hunter before speaking to Mirja. "Oh, he did. And it was most delicious, but I couldn't eat half as much as I wanted to. It was all I could do to finish my plate."

"Hm," Mirja replied. "Well, if you are to be an acolyte, we must get you a brown cassock. You can have one of my old ones. I was but ten when I came here. It should fit you well enough, once you start eating."

"Mirja," Hunter interjected wearily. He was ignored.

"Now, he can teach you how to ride and hunt and fight, but I have still sense enough to teach you embroidery, spinning, and healing, of course, but that goes without saying for an acolyte."

"Mirja," Hunter said again.

"He said he would teach me to read," Sinopa said with a smile. It was difficult not to get carried away by this woman's joyful enthusiasm.

"Read? Yes, I suppose there must be someone here to read. Old Jarvis used to take care of the books, but he has been dead for a long time now. You will be busy."

"Mirja!" Hunter snapped, drawing the old woman's attention at last. She arched her brows at him. "She is a guest, and no more."

"Well," Mirja said rather sourly, "we must need to please our guests. Would you like to learn how to embroider and spin and heal?"

Sinopa wasn't sure she wanted to, but was so delighted by Mirja's enthusiasm, and felt so safe in this house, away from the city guard and the brutal life of the street that she nodded. "Very much so."

"And would you like to be taught how to hunt and ride and fight, also?"

"Oh yes!"

Mirja turned to Hunter. "Well?" she demanded.

Hunter's shoulders slumped in defeat. "Very well," he agreed. "However, she stays as a guest. Nothing is expected of her, Mirja, and don't go telling secrets, either."

"Cross my heart," Mirja replied in a tone that said the exact opposite.

"Indeed," Hunter rumbled irritably. "I shall leave you both, then. If you are lost, Sinopa, simply utter your desired destination, and the way will be lit."

"Thank you," Sinopa said sincerely. "For everything."

Hunter simply grunted and left, taking his hounds with him.

"Big old grump," Mirja scoffed. She took up her cutlery. "Sit child, and tell me all about yourself."

Sinopa sat and related her tale in full to Mirja as the woman ate. At times she had to fight back tears as she recalled the events that led to her life as a common petty thief.

"And then," she finished, "I stumbled inside, and found myself a guest to a man in a hooded cloak."

Mirja almost snorted food out her nose and she looked at Sinopa with arched brows. "A man indeed," she muttered. "Have they all forgotten?"

Sinopa knew that question was not for her, so she did not reply.

"What name did he give you?" Mirja asked her.

"Hunter," Sinopa replied.

"Hunter?" Mirja said with a laugh. "Oh indeed! Hunter! The first and the last."

Sinopa stared at her blankly.

"Never mind, child," Mirja said with a smile.

Sinopa yawned, though tried hard to hide it.

"Well now, I've been starved of company for so many years I've gone and forgotten my manners. You must go to bed, child. There will be plenty of time to talk on the morrow."

"But..."

"No buts! Even curious minds must rest. Now go."

"Yes, Mirja." Sinopa left the room and found herself in a dark tunnel. She could not see, let alone hope to find her room. "Bed," she whispered. A torch to her right sprang to life with a guttering hiss, the torch further down doing the same, until all the torches from here to her bedchamber were lit. With a smile, Sinopa followed the lit torches to gratefully sink into bed.

It was pitch black when she opened her eyes next. She did not know the time, but guessed that it must be close to midnight. She was still tired, but restless. She slipped from the sheets and walked out to the tunnel.

"Hunter," she whispered and the torches sprang to life. She followed them until she found herself in the library once more. Hunter was on his obsidian throne, putting an ink-laden quill to a page in a massive tome. His hounds snoozed at his feet. He looked up in surprise as the candles flickered to life.

"Sinopa."

"Will you read me a story?" Sinopa asked. Her father used to read her bedtime stories, and she would fall asleep listening to the sound of his voice. Sleeping in a bed without being told a story seemed wrong.

Hunter hesitated a moment before he put down his quill and blew on the page he had been working on. He flipped the book open to the first page and held out his hands to Sinopa, who ran gratefully into them. He lifted her up onto his lap and wrapped her into the folds of his cloak.

"This is the tale of Sreng," he said, his deep voice soothing and distant. Sinopa smiled and settled herself down.

Hunter went on to tell the story. He spoke of a people, the First Men, he called them, who lived on an island and were peaceful. Then came the Second Men, and they were not peaceful. The Second Men tried to take away the land from the First Men and keep it for themselves. It meant war. In this war, fought Sreng, a war-leader of the First Men, unrivalled in intelligence and skill.

The First Men did not know about iron, and fought with weapons of wood and stone and bronze. The Second Men had swords of steel. Even so, so cunning and able was the war-leader Sreng that the war ended in a stalemate.

As part of the terms of truce, the island was split in half. One half went to the First Men, the other to the Second Men. The First Men could not step foot onto the half of the island owned by the Second Men without first becoming animals except twice yearly. The same was true of the Second Men, but since the First Men were the only ones who knew how to change forms, the Second Men never ventured into the lands of the First Men except by chance, and few ever made it back.

So impressed with Sreng were the Second Men, that he and he alone was invited to share with them the bounty of their half of the island. On behalf of the First Men, Sreng accepted to act as liaison and arbiter between the two groups of men.

He became a king of the Second Men, and the only one of the First Men to ever be able to unconditionally step foot on both sides of the island without consequence. His name became a thing of legend that was remembered for a long, long time, but, Hunter concluded sadly, is now forgotten.

Sinopa had fallen asleep long before Hunter had concluded his tale. Even so, her dreams were filled with each scene Hunter described, and she could recall them ever after. Hunter looked down at the sleeping child in his arms and sighed.

"My poor little fox," he said. He carefully set aside the tome he had been reading from, and lifted Sinopa up. Careful not to wake her, he carried her back to her bed and tucked her in.

"Sleep well," he said before leaving the room.

Sinopa spent her days in continual wonderment at all she did not know, and all she was being shown. Her days living on the streets served her well in combat lessons, and she showed great promise in dagger and short sword. She loved archery most of all, however, and when she was skilled enough, she combined her riding lessons with her archery lessons.

There was but one horse left in the stable to learn to ride. Hunter's own stallion, black from head to hoof, with a temperament as dark as its coat. Even still, Sinopa loved the beast. After a few false starts, the horse came to love her also. She loved to ride. Hunter's horse, also called Hunter, could run like the wind, and would take Sinopa on long gallops, leaving her breathless and delighted.

It seemed that the back garden stretched on into eternity. Sinopa wondered how it could be so, since the house was located in the heart of the city

There was a small forest in the back garden in which grew every herb and fungus imaginable. Mirja would shuffle through the forest with Sinopa in tow, teaching her how to recognise each plant, and what they could be used for. Sinopa learnt quickly, and became a skilled healer. So skilled a healer, in fact, that Mirja would soon come to rely on her for making the teas to soothe the wracking cough that plagued the old woman.

Sinopa would take every meal with Hunter, excluding lunch, which Hunter did not eat. She would take her lunches with Mirja instead and the two would exchange tales. Laughter, not heard in the tunnels for an age, would ring all the way to the library, where Hunter was diligently working. He would smile as he worked, but it was a smile tinged with sadness, for Mirja's health was failing and soon no tincture would avail her.

For all this, Mirja was more active in the house than she had been for a long while. She would leave her room and watch Sinopa training, cackling with raucous laughter every time Hunter was bested (a rare occurrence indeed), or cheering when Sinopa hit her mark dead on (not rare at all). For a time, at least, it was as if they were family.

As it is with all children, however, Sinopa would not stop growing. It seemed but a few days in this house before she had turned sixteen. Like her mother before her, Sinopa was a stunningly beautiful young woman, with long locks of shining deep red hair and bright grey eyes that sparkled.

Sinopa seemed unaware that she was changing, but for Hunter the awareness was painful. The innocent kisses on the cheek that Sinopa gave him before bed were now difficult to return with the same innocent intent. Shortly before her seventeenth birthday, though she had long lost track of birthdays, Hunter could bear it no longer.

He seemed tense and distant as Sinopa wished him a good night and though Sinopa frowned, she did not raise the issue. It was with a surprised flush of pleasure that she noted he watched her carefully as she left. The surprise was all the more greater when she realised that knowing that his eyes were on her gave her such pleasure. She slipped into bed that evening with a smile on her face.

Hunter was not as content. He paced furiously in his room before approaching the mirror kept above his washbasin. He pulled back his hood and studied his reflection. He was so unlike the men that surrounded his house now.

Hunter was like all men of his people had been, though some would swear he was more handsome. His skin was a warm golden brown, his angular eyes bright green. His jet-black hair was tied in a neat plait that fell down his back, the end of which was affixed with feathers, in the tradition of his people. High cheekbones dominated his features.

For all his years, he still looked young. Only the slight touch of grey at his temples hinted at any advancement in age, and even those had remained unchanged for eons. He wondered idly if Sinopa would find him handsome, then sighed at himself in frustration. "You are a fool," he told his reflection before he replaced his hood and made his quiet way to the library. "It is time."

Sinopa woke the following morning and dressed in her riding clothes. Hunter had made her riding boots for her, and her archer's brace. She loved them very much and would sometimes wear them for the sheer pleasure of wearing them. She stepped outside into the dark tunnel and said, "Stables."

Nothing happened.

Sinopa frowned. She would not be able to find her way in the dark.

"Stables," she said again a little louder. Still there was nothing. "Come on now," she muttered. "Stables."

This time the torches lit, though to her left, not her right as they normally did when she went to the stables. Frowning, Sinopa followed the path of light slowly and found herself in the library. It was deserted and unlit but for the daylight that streamed through the open bronze doors. Sinopa gasped.

She walked to the doorway and stopped staring out at the brightness of early afternoon. In the front garden, happily grazing was Hunter's horse, Hunter. He wore his tack, and more, he carried all the weapons that Hunter had given Sinopa. Though she knew what this meant, she refused the sign. She stepped backwards, right into Hunter, and he wrapped his arms around her and pulled her close as tears streamed down her cheeks.

"It is time, Sinopa," he said gently.

Sinopa turned around. "I don't want to go," she whispered.

"I know."

"Please, don't make me."

Hunter took Sinopa by her shoulders. "I am dying, Sinopa," he told her.

"And when I am gone, there will be no one to care for you. It is time for you to find your path, and walk it."

Sinopa was struck dumb by the revelation. "Dying? What? How?"

"It does not matter now."

"But..."

"Hush," Hunter soothed, pressing one finger against Sinopa's tear-stained lips. He drew from his pocket Sinopa's pouch and withdrew her mother's ring from it. Taking her right hand, he slid the ring onto her finger.

"Go into the forest," he told her. "There is a group of men there who will welcome you."

"No," Sinopa gulped, shaking her head. "Please."

"You cannot stay, Sinopa."

"I want to stay. I want to stay here. With you."

"I know." Hunter stroked Sinopa's pale cheek. Against his better judgement, he kissed that cheek, and did not care for the lack of innocence in the act. Sobbing, Sinopa threw her arms around him and Hunter returned the embrace. He held her until she could no longer cry.

"I love you," Sinopa whispered.

"And I you."

They kissed. It was a lingering kiss; gentle and sad. At length, Hunter pulled away. "Now you must leave," he said.

Sinopa, tears threatening again, nodded. "I shall never forget you."

Hunter smiled sadly, but said nothing. He felt her pull away from him, and it was all he could do not to pull her back. She turned abruptly and strode out into the sun, her hair glistening like spun garnet. She mounted the horse and walked him slowly to the bronze gates, which opened with a groan.

There she paused and Hunter hoped that she might turn, that he would look upon her face one last time. But she did not turn. She urged the horse forward through the gate. Hunter heard the sound of a horse at gallop grow distant before the groan of the garden gates overpowered the sound.

The creaking complaint of the heavy bronze doors of the house added to the chorus of straining metal of the outside gate as they slowly pulled closed. They banged into place with a deep, echoing boom. Hunter reached out and pressed his palm against the door.

"Good luck, little fox," he murmured.

"You are an idiot," Mirja said in disgust at the tunnel entrance before turning and hobbling down the hall.

"She could not stay, Mirja," Hunter said quietly.

"I know that!" Mirja snapped, then she sighed. "She loved you, my Lord."

"And I her."

Mirja sighed again. "My cane is not enough now. Will you help me back to my room?"

"Of course."

Mirja died before the dawn. Her lord sat with her through the long night, making her tonics to ease the discomfort of her coughing. He even sang to her; an old song, a song of the First Men, one his mother sung to him when he was still a child.

When Mirja's last breath left her, Hunter sang on, grief making his voice throaty. He carried her out to the forest she had loved so much and dug there a shallow grave. He lay her down and, after kissing her brow, covered her over. He then went to his private chambers and gathered the few belongings he felt he would still desire.

His sword, broken halfway down the blade in battle against the then high king, a thick golden torque, a gift from that very same king at the battle's conclusion, and his battle helm, a thick leather cap reinforced by bronze bands, upon which were affixed a pair of antlers from a breed of deer made extinct long ago by careless hunting.

His hood had a special space where the antlers could protrude without him having to reveal his face. Pulling on his leather gloves, he strode from the house. "You are now Sinopa's," he told the house as he left. "You open only for her."

With nothing left there for him, Hunter left the garden and walked tall up the alley, and through the city. He stood a head and shoulders taller than the tallest person in the city, and though many stared at him with wide, frightened eyes, no one dared impede him. Not even the heavily armed city guard, who had, just moments ago, been arresting a farmer for daring to imply that the rightful owner of the castle had galloped through the market not a day ago.

He walked out of the city, and through farmland, with strong, purposeful strides. The land had changed much since last he had stepped foot outside. Yet he knew where to go. He walked on, passed the pastureland and deep into the forest. He arrived just as the sun was setting.

The Hunter's Throne, they called it, though none now remembered why. The rain and wind had turned the throne into nothing more than a vaguely chair-shaped formation. It had once been exquisitely carved.

He had sat in that throne as a man, after he had been made a king of the Second Men. He would sit and watch the yearly festival held in his honour. Girls would dance, and jesters would tell tales and jokes. Musicians played and people feasted. That had been a lifetime ago, when Hunter was a young man, and a hero.

Hunter observed the throne. Where once it sat on a small hill overlooking broad plains, it now was hidden amidst tall bracken and shrouded by forest. With a sigh, Hunter sat on the throne, letting his arms relax onto what was left of the armrests. He straightened in the seat and closed his weary eyes. He was cold. Even the orange sun burning between the trunks of trees could do nothing to warm his rapidly cooling skin.

"And now," he whispered. "I die."

Sinopa was not sure where she was going, or why, but she trusted Hunter and so continued to walk her horse along the trail in the woods. It had been three days and she had seen no one. She was on that very thought when rocks tumbled down from an overhang. She stopped her horse dead and looked about her.

"Well, now you've done it!" she heard someone grumble. A smile twitched at her lips. A clumsy ambush indeed. Her hand went to her sword and she withdrew it. The bronze gleamed. She had no time to marvel at it, however. Men appeared on all sides. They were ragged of appearance, with a desperate light in their eyes.

"What are you going to do with that?" one man sneered.

"Come closer and find out," Sinopa snapped.

"Oh, a mouthy noble are you? Well, we'll take good care of that."

"You will not lay a hand on me," Sinopa replied, more bravely than she felt.

The men laughed sinisterly.

"Who are you?" Sinopa demanded.

"Us?" one man said with false innocence. "We are the king's men, traitor."

Sinopa gave a start and she looked at the man in surprise. Grey hair and leaner features made him difficult to recognise, but the captain of the earl's guard he was nonetheless. Sinopa smiled a little.

"Marshal?" she asked timidly.

The man, who had been advancing, stopped dead. "How do you know my name?"

"Marshal," Sinopa said quietly. "I am Sinopa."

The man eyed her suspiciously. "Sinopa is dead. She died with the rest."

"No," Sinopa said quietly. "I was disguised as a serving girl and escaped the attack on the castle. My mother gave me her ring." She removed her riding glove and extended her right hand so the man named Marshal could see.

"Very pretty," one man snorted. "Now give that here and we just might not slit your throat."

"Shut it, Mark," Marshal snapped. He took Sinopa's hand and examined the ring. "If that's a fake it's well done," he conceded at length.

Sinopa could have laughed. "It is not fake. Perhaps I look older than I feel, and so you do not recognise me, but I remember you leading my pony when father would go to hunt, and I wanted to watch."

Marshal looked up at Sinopa in wonder. "My Lady," he said thickly.

"Father," a smooth, deep voice said from ahead. Sinopa and Marshal both turned to see a young man, holding a brace of rabbits in one hand and a bow in the other. He was older than Sinopa by three years, perhaps, and was handsome indeed. Dark hair fell about his shoulders in gentle waves, and bright brown eyes watched the scene over prominent cheekbones. His skin was tanned brown by a life lived out of doors. Sinopa was caught immediately.

"What's the hold up?"

"My son, come here. Come here and meet our hope. My Lady Sinopa, this is my son Victor."

"Sinopa?" Victor said in awe. "*The* Sinopa. Annoying little Sinopa who would not shut up?"

"Victor!"

Sinopa laughed. "The same, Victor. I remember you now. I followed you all day like a shadow."

"Aye, and wouldn't stop chattering."

Sinopa nodded and smiled.

"My Lady," Marshal said. "We have an army hidden in these woods, and contacts all over the country. We are ready for revolt."

"Please," Sinopa said gently. "I have been travelling three days without rest. Will you permit me some time by a fire and food?"

"Yes, of course!" Marshal said. He held out his hands to help Sinopa from her horse, but she needed no assistance. She dismounted lithely and smiled at Marshal.

"Are all those weapons yours?" Victor asked Sinopa.

"Of course," Sinopa replied, sheathing her bronze sword.

"A bronze sword?"

"Yes, perhaps the very same bronze sword that belonged to Sreng, defender of the First Men."

"Well that sounds like a tale worth hearing. Will you tell it?"

"So I shall, after my meal." And she did.

Not very far away, at the heart of a formless lump of stone they called The Hunter's Throne, a small flush of heat began its slow spread.

Fin.

Special Edition

Become a starling https://ko-fi.com/smcarriere and get access to an all new special edion of *The Dying God*, with all new art from the author

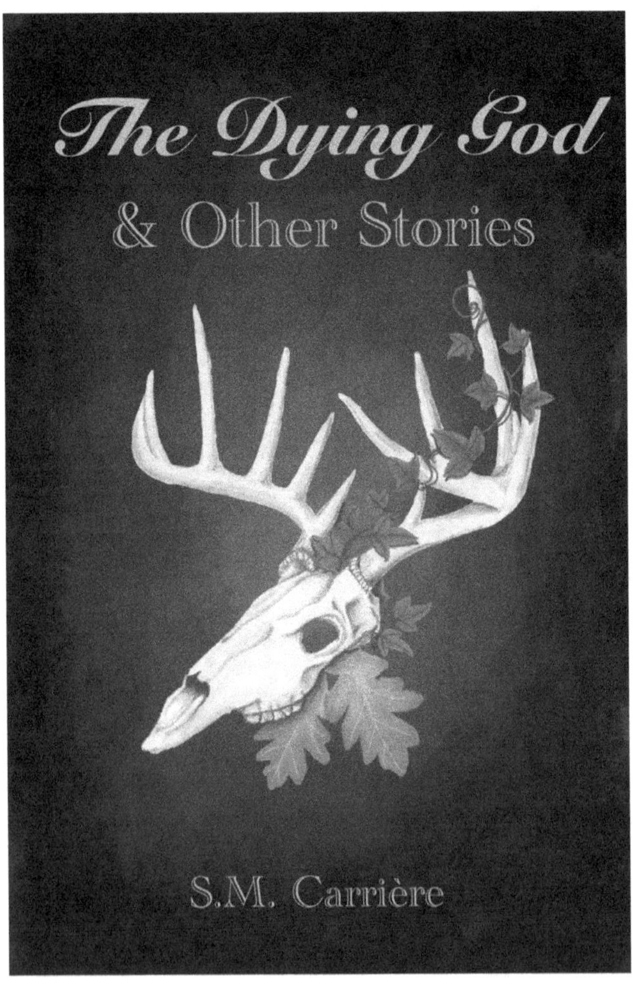

About the Author

When S.M. Carrière isn't brutally killing your favourite characters, she spends her time teaching martial arts, live streaming video games, occasionally teaching at the University of Ottawa, and cuddling her cat. In other words, she spends her time teaching others to kill, streaming her digital kills, teaching about historical death, and cuddling a furry murderer.

Want to join the community? Perks include early access to videos, blog posts and updates as well as subscriber exclusive book editions and other treats, and the warm, fuzzy feeling of helping an independent author.

Become a Starling at https://ko-fi.com/smcarriere.

More by S.M. Carrière

Ethan Cadfael: The Battle Prince

The Summer Bird (The Seraphimé Saga, v. 1)

The Winter Wolf (The Seraphimé Saga, v. 2)

Skyroad Walker

Daughters of Britain

Skylark

Human

The New Haven Incident

www.ingramcontent.com/pod-product-compliance
Lightning Source LLC
Chambersburg PA
CBHW070555180626
46817CB00005B/1858

* 9 7 8 0 9 9 3 8 5 0 9 9 8 *